Hairdresser on Fire

Hairdresser on Fire

a novel

Manic D Press
San Francisco

Dedicated
to
Joel Casey
my favorite human, with all of my love, always

Cover photo by Joel Casey

Hairdresser on Fire ©2013 by Daniel LeVesque. All rights reserved.
Published by Manic D Press. For information, contact Manic D Press,
PO Box 410804, San Francisco CA 94141   www.manicdpress.com
ISBN 978-1-933149-73-8   printed in the USA
Cataloging-in-Publication data is on file with the Library of Congress

For Sammy

I

Despite what has been written on countless salon applications, I cannot say with any stitch of truth that my childhood dream was to express myself through hairstyling. It's all a lie. There was never any burning desire to *do hair* — not to touch it, arrange it, or place adjectives in front of it, e.g., *overprocessed* or *silky* hair.

If you ask, you'll often hear the story told in a mystical way. Ramón will tell you, "I was doing hair in all of my lifetimes," spinning his hand above his head, a halo of tracers orbiting his hairdo, opal black eyes turned skyward (trust I am not poking fun at the Ramóns of the world. I adore the Ramóns; without the Ramóns, I am nothing). But, unlike The Ramóns, hair was not my calling in grade school, and falling into it was nothing more than random cosmic career assignment. I could just as well be repairing people's air conditioners today, or drawing their blood. Massaging their thighs. A Trade. The sun eats itself.

At eleven years old, my Grand Purpose, my calling, was to be a circus clown and a stuntman, merging the two into one glamorous pratfalling career. Dick Van Dyke tried it but not on the scale that I'd envisioned.

My father loved *The Dick Van Dyke Show*. In the opening, Dick would walk in and trip over this hassock, and every time my dad would crack up like he never saw it coming. He'd laugh so hard that no noise came out, lying on his belly in front of the teevee with me sprawled over his back like a little monkey. When he'd laugh so hard he was like a ride at the fair, his back heaving silent screams of laughter, me flopping back and forth until I cracked up too. I always found comfort in the laughter of my father. For me, it wasn't about the hassock at all.

After a few seasons of the show, the opening changed. Dick Van Dyke would come in, *act* like he was going to trip over the hassock, and then do a near miss, jump-over-the-hassock gag. Upon landing, there was this little steppy tap dance number he did, mincing and grinning real proud. The clever side of the Fool. My father didn't laugh at the beginning anymore so he would get up, tossing me into the deep shag, and change the channel. He liked that hassock bit a lot. He sure did miss it. This would not be the summer that my father got sober. *Thanks a bunch, Dick.*

Other than wanting to slam Dick Van Dyke's long face into the cement wall of our cellar, I wanted clown props, and would have traded all the giant honking horns in the world for a set of clown make-up. Becoming a clown without proper make-up is difficult at best, a possible reason for so much sadness and alcoholism present in the clown community: Repressed Childhood Make-Up Memories. No mother wants their son to love clowns, let alone be one.

As Clown Children we are marked, and for this we are forced to dig, to find a way to make it happen. Unlike the way Theater People start out — jazzy adolescents in Drama Club, scrawling loopy "See ya on Broadways!!!" in senior yearbooks — Child Clowns have no such reception. We must learn early to make our childhoods work or to break them ourselves. Nobody reaches out to help a kid who wears suspenders so we chew holes in the box.

In lieu of owning a tube of Clown White, I used a lotion/talcum powder recipe. Oh, coveted Clown White, with your perfect consistency and shocking opacity. I could eat you, the way I eat my sister's cherry-flavored Bonne Bell lip gloss. I need you. I never get you.

My mother's top dresser drawer only collected things I couldn't use for painting my face. Ketchup packets from Burger Chef, single use salts and peppers, old samples of beauty products that she would never consider putting on her face or throwing away, empty matchbooks — these are the items she hung on to.

Medium-brown Maybelline stick was the only make-up option

among the riffraff that filled my mother's dresser. I used it for lips, eyes, and teardrops. The lack of rouge pushed me dangerously close to mime territory so I did what I could with what I had. How To:

1) Begin by applying a light layer of Mary Kay lotion over the entire face.

2) Wait until it almost stops stinging.

3) Pat mounds of talcum over the sticky lotion.

4) Drag the scratchy Maybelline medium-brown pencil around eyes and lips until skin tears and bleeds, creating a total look.

Results were most often clumpy but after a few applications a sufficient washed-out pallor would take over my face, flaking like oats within an hour as I jumped off the garage in the summertime for stuntman practice. A ruby red lipstick was my only saving grace and I used it sparingly, saving it for serious clown shows or when pictures would be taken. It was a full tube but I knew better than to waste it. If I had to name the color, it would be "Mercy." The tube came from the house next door where I could sometimes get lucky, hoping my neighbor would toss me a lipstick she didn't like during spring cleaning.

"Take this one, hon. It's Mary Kay SHIT," Betsy would say. She was allergic to Mary Kay, as was my mother. But my mother didn't have any lipsticks hanging around, just the ketchups. Betsy had so many lipsticks she didn't use anymore, all reds. I would have run away to next-door for the simple promise of a discarded lipstick once in a while, maybe some proper concealer. I always wanted to live with our neighbors, the Pagans, right next door and a thousand miles away. Bobby, Betsy, Marty, and Jennifer. The Pagans.

Bobby Pagan watched a lot of teevee and stuff — it was always on for some sports show — but their house had a different feeling, a different smell: the smell of burning electricity from the all the teevees running in empty rooms, the smell of ovens preheating and cold cardboard under frozen pizza. The Pagans didn't hide their empty wine bottles or wash the red rings of cheap Port from the bottoms of their glasses before going to bed. The Pagans fought and didn't make up, they went to bed mad. The Pagans said *fuck*.

I tried to be there as much as I could, as Betsy Pagan had all the best clown shades in her make-up box but, God, if she caught me in her room without permission she would throw a bottle at my head. Betsy collected bottles, always having a head-smasher within arm's reach. She would grab for the heaviest bottle, the one with all the quarters in it, to whip at my head. It must have had a hundred bucks in it. Don't think I wasn't eyeballing that one, either. Its coins could have bought my bus ticket to clown school and back. It was one of those wine bottles from Italy, wrapped in its own wicker basket by children with nubby fingers. You could hang it up.

There were bottles with wax dripped down them in colorful layers, years of flaming candles formed into mounds, the wax so thick on some of them that there was only a hint of the original bottle's shape left behind. Some of the bottles had shells in them. Shells and sea glass stomped into pieces so Betsy could cram them down the neck of the bottle. My mom said that Betsy only filled all those bottles because she had so much fun emptying them. A lot of the time my mom breaks her own "if you can't say anything nice…" rule. Sometimes you have to.

Betsy would spend hours ripping up tiny pieces of masking tape and sticking them to the emptied Blue Nun bottles, until every inch of glass was covered for all the tape. Magical faux finishes appeared when she began rubbing over the tape with shoe polish on a paper towel. It created this cracked brown look over the surface, dark in some places, lighter in others, and I must admit that even I was a little taken aback by the results.

"Betsy, I love that one over there. The one with the dark brown shoe polish all on the tape."

"It's sable brown," she'd say. "The shoe polish. *Sable*. Like my hair." Betsy's hair was flat-tire black, nothing at all like the chocolaty brown shoe polish shining off the bottle in the corner. She acted like she invented it, too, this whole tape and shoe polish process, not wanting to share her medium with the world. Activities such as tape-rubbing are supposed to make old people happy, or give schoolchildren something accessible to create. When crafts are elevated and held to any sort of standards, the whole world suffers (witness the bonsai community).

Betsy would soon be involved in macramé, a then emerging form involving knotting pieces of twine into patterns. Once she was convinced that her style of knotting twine was exclusive to her, Betsy began fashioning macramé bottle holders. It was the next logical evolution of her talents, creating new places to put new bottles. Once a year she sold the completed pieces at BraätFest, a local French-Canadian church bazaar with a dubious Germanic moniker.

The artisans who rented BraätFest booths sold an assortment of crocheted toilet paper cozies, shouting wooden WELCOME! signs, potpourri baskets and — for the first time this year — macramé art. Betsy sold the most with her bottle holders. Seems a lot of people at church needed a place to put their empty bottles and dressing them up in waxy twine was the perfect idea.

My mother never attended a church bazaar on principle but would always volunteer to clean up after. She would be furious, scratching at a piece of scotch tape stuck to the nose of a statue of Saint Agatha. "Jesus smashed the temple in *Jesus Christ Superstar* because people were making money in God's house, remember? All those girls were dancing, remember? And the drugs and the guns and the mirrors! All in His Father's house! Jesus was so mad, so mad He smashed the mirrors!"

Everything I believe about Christianity is from the movie *Jesus Christ Superstar*; it's a good reference point.

"Jesus said, 'Not in my Father's house, you don't! No way, José!' and Jesus flipped those tables and yelled at those vendors, 'Get out! Get ouuuut!' he says. Remember? Same thing with the bingo. And these goddamn church bazaars." She looked around when she said *goddamn* to see if anyone witnessed her breaking the third commandment.

Blasphemy is big in my family of devout Catholics, especially the older ones. They took these phrases with them from Canada, these insane combinations of words. Phrases that reached the height of irreverence, these little Canuck sacrileges that flew out of my grandmother's mouth. *"Eee, Mutarde si marde Tabernak," "Ah, siboire,"* and *"Eee, Crisse,"* were spoken from the safety of her La-Z-Boy without fear of heavenly repercussion.

I didn't know what the words meant as a kid but, roughly translated, Memere and Ma Tantes were saying things like "Mustard shits on the tabernacle," and "Shit on the Holy Host!" with zero regard for the third or fourth commandments. My parents said "Mutard si merde," and "Ah, siboire," all the time and when I would ask what the words meant they would tell me, "It means 'mustard seeds.' But don't say it." To this day, I don't say mustard seeds.

My mother was kneeling at Saint Agatha's feet with a dust rag, wiping between the cemented folds of her hem. "Eee mutard si merde. Jesus would flip these tables if He knew what was going on in here… but He knows. Oh, Heeee knows… People playing roulette in the house of God. Gambling!" She was right. I wanted to flip the stupid tables myself. It was all so bright and finicky, covered by the smell of church basement coffee percolators being emptied, their insides scrubbed with church basement cleaning liquid and steel wool.

"And Betsy Pagan! Oh, I'm sure *she's* gonna give ten percent back to the church with her stupid bottles, I mean, who couldn't do that? I could do that! Wax on bottles? *Stupid*. And it only gets everywhere, see? Look… look… I mean, it got all over Saint Agatha's basement floor, that's all I know. Goddam bottles." She looked up to the eyes of the statue, little home-permed curls pressed in sweaty rings around her forehead. "Oh, Saint Agatha, as if you didn't have to see enough suffering already," she said, crossing herself once before standing, then again right after. "They cut her tits off, ya know."

My mother didn't know about Betsy's macramé bottle holders yet, and I wasn't going to be the one to tell her. She was convinced that the Pagans were up to something at all times because they didn't have a crucifix hanging in their house or a picture of a lamb or anything. Just the bottles. "And that lipstick!" my mother would say, and I would always know the exact shade Betsy had on that day. "That lipstick! S-L-U-T R-E-D, that's the shade."

The same Slut Red I dreamed of stealing, to stain a smile onto the inch of skin surrounding my mouth, allowing for entrance to the school of my dreams. *I will get in*, I thought every day as I waited for the mailman to come with my information packet.

The application form for the Ringling Bros. and Barnum & Bailey Clown College is the same form used for evaluating patients before admitting them to psychiatric hospitals.

The written evaluation begins innocently enough, lulling you into a clown-ready state, a rubber-nosed frenzy of fantasy and longing, before they slam you with the hard questions. (There must be some sort of practical exam done later, after you've wowed them with your credentials on paper.)

The full-color catalog of classes they sent had course titles that damn near killed me from anxiety. *Intro to Pratfalling with Professor Stumbly. Advanced Team Juggling with Miss Scorchy. Stilting 101 with Clementine Shorty.* Judging by the pictures, student clowns went everywhere on stilts, bright smiles beaming through painted frowns.

Their make-up was high quality product expertly applied and I would've killed them for it given the chance. Glossy candid shots exposed the student clowns in their off time: combing their wigs, drinking out of cans, stilting around with red rubber balls that swirled in the background of every picture. In their breakfast photo they were eating noodles; I wanted to join them immediately.

After licking the pen tip real hard, I started filling out the application for my life.

NAME: Francis Stewart Plinkin/ Zilcho the Clown — I wasn't sure if they needed my real name or my clown name, so I put both.

AGE: 18 — I put eighteen instead of eleven. I didn't want to scare them off with my youth before I had the chance to win them over in person. Age wasn't a worry, as Institutions of Higher Learning were beginning to appreciate the genius of youth. All over the news, on teevee, on *That's Incredible!*, there were eleven-year-olds in post-graduate schools, preteen geniuses performing microsurgery and shattering ageist constructs, but these were the rich kids at Johns Hopkins Medical. Clown colleges most likely had a different take on early entry programs for geniuses. I licked the tip of the pen again, something I saw my dad do, and got serious. I didn't even put on a full costume.

HOW MANY TIMES HAVE YOU MOVED IN THE LAST 10 YEARS? — There was the once, out of the project and two streets over to the tenement but I didn't remember it. "Six times," I wrote in my best handwriting. Logically, they would be seeking someone driven, with a penchant for travel, not some dead weight balloon-twister who'd be content to work the local birthday party circuit for the rest of his life. "Six times" should properly amaze the admissions clowns without going over the top.

HOW MANY JOBS HAVE YOU HELD IN THE PAST 10 YEARS? — "Six." Obvious. I was on a roll. Willing to work. After a few more questions about the basics — location, gender, citizenship — I moved on to the next section where the innocence wore clean off.

The psycho-social part of the application was a mind-boggling collection of questions pertaining to abuse, buggery, IV drug use, and prison records. I laid myself on the floor, pressing my cheek to the shag until composure took me back to a place of readiness.

Marty Pagan and his friends were playing outside, giggling and chatting as I sat with my application. They were talking about me. *Bottomfeeders.* See what they say about me in six months when I'm famous and they're going nowhere. So what if I can't play hockey? Those helmets give me a headache and I don't see any of them applying to colleges. *Okay, focus.* The pen was sweating in my hand and I was craving make-up.

HAVE YOU BEEN CONVICTED OF A FELONY IN THE LAST 10 YEARS? — "No." Bonnie Beleau forced me to steal bath beads from Mammoth Mart once but I got away with it so I'm sure there's no record. It was all Bonnie's idea. She practically stuck them down my pants. Before I knew it, I was shoplifting, Bonnie going "Come on, come on," the whole time and me, guilty as hell — I was sure they'd catch me — flushed and anxious as I passed the giant elephant who guarded the door. We popped the bath beads with our feet in the parking lot.

HAVE YOU EVER BEEN CONVICTED OF A SEX CRIME? — Sex crimes! This was too much. Sex and crime in one question. I was eleven. What did they mean? I put "N/A" which my sister told me meant "No Answer."

I tore through the rest of the application to see if there were any questions about juggling, rolling out the barrel, make-up application/removal, or any of the things I practiced every day. Nothing. Must be in the practical.

Page three was all about drugs. I put N/A in all the drug question boxes. If only I had been filling this out six years later, I would have been able to fill page three front and back, opening up my chances for full scholarship.

HAVE YOU EVER BEEN CONVICTED OF MOLESTING A CHILD? — Oh, my dear Lord. Wouldn't that fall under sex crimes? I was going to put "No Answer," but then I thought of how me and Scoot Ryder would kiss every day behind the garage. Real Hollywood kisses, our lips tight and our faces pressed together hard. I thought of the first time he parted my lips with his tongue; we were frenching. His mouth tasted like the Swedish Fish penny candies he had eaten on the walk over to my house, his tongue a film of red gelatin.

Our relationship lasted all through junior high, where Scoot was the reigning Metal God. He had a tattoo, a fucking tattoo in seventh grade. I would have followed him around with a mattress strapped to my back if I could've. When it came time to move from frenching to third base, Scoot got scared. "Won't that make us gay?"

"Make us gay? What are you talking about?" I answered all of his questions with questions for years, keeping everything simple like we were making toast. Scoot was easy to distract. Technically we were both minors when our affair began in grade school but there were no arrests or convictions so I just wrote NO. To eliminate all doubt, I added an exclamation point. NO!

DO YOU HAVE ANY TATTOOS? — In the mirror I saw the stars scratched on to my cheeks in medium-brown mascara. "No."

WHAT'S THE LONGEST YOU'VE BEEN IN PRISON? — The presumption that I was, of course, a former inmate seemed like a trick question so I put "N/A." This process was so intense but I knew it had to be and I was willing to give them what they wanted. There has to be an initial screening process in place in order to weed out the good clowns (like Willie Whistle), from the bad clowns (like John Wayne Gacy).

My signature signed, I stuffed the finished questionnaire into an envelope, minus the $75.00 check for the non-refundable application fee. My mom said, "No way," when I asked her for the money, despite the passion of my begging. "Mom, please! This is my life we're talking about!" The "this is my life…" part was in a movie, so I used it.

In the movie, it worked; Judith Light's character screamed, "This is MY life!" to the ex-husband character who caved immediately upon hearing the words. The magic phrase didn't work on my mother. I forgot we had watched the movie together and that she hated Judith Light way more than she hated clowns.

She was not budging on the application fee even if it was my life. She got real close to my face, very serious. "Clowns have miserable lives, Francis. Clowns die drunk and alone in their big shoes." That was it. My mother had put her fears to their finest point.

I guess parents don't dream that their kids will be clowns. My mom and all her sisters wanted me to be a priest, and told me that God had chosen me for the cloth. She meant it, too. The priesthood.

"You were meant to be a priest," she insisted. "Father Hazebrook said so. A clown, Francis? No way. No way am I bloodying my hands with your demise." Suddenly she was Pontius Pilate, washing her hands in an imaginary bowl she kept on her vanity, miming as she railed against clowns, using my own weapons against me. "A clown! My God, Francis." She started to fan herself with a magazine, real dramatic. I think the "bloodied hands" number was in a movie, too, a Jesus movie she saw.

She acted as if she knew a whole bunch of clowns before she'd met my dad. As if her teen life was filled with unexpected shaving-cream pies to the face. Even now she shivers when someone mentions clowning. So does my sister, all of her friends, and most of the kids at school. "Oh, clowns scare me to death!" my sister always said at the Macy's Thanksgiving Day parade when we were dragged up Fifth Avenue every year, exhausted and late from the three-hour drive, but she's not dead yet.

It's hip to act fearful of clowns and most Americans are not coulrophobes, they're compulsive liars. Clown hate is cool and runs unchecked in our society. If a clown molested you, okay then, clowning may not be your favorite form of entertainment. Getting diddled by a pervert in pointy make-up is a valid reason to harbor clown hate, and you should run from them for the rest of your life. Or you could face their sad painted faces head on and confront your fears. Whatever helps you sleep at night. I, personally, run to sedation rather than confrontation, but don't listen to me. Seriously.

My mother, a notorious clown bigot, told me again that she would rather slice her face than give me the $75 application fee, enabling me to throw my life away. Then she started the miming again: slicing at her face with a butter knife, checking her wallet, and wiping away tears. She was good at it, using props and everything. Maybe she had her own broken dream of clowning before she handed her life over to the textile mills when she was twelve.

Everybody worked in one factory or another here, assembling pieces of parts that would go on to become the sole of a shoe or the fin of a rocket. I liked thinking that my mom built rockets but she didn't. She built shoe soles.

Her mother before her worked in a knitting mill, loading yarn in repetitive motion onto large spools to be shipped. In her last years on earth, this repetitive motion was all she could remember. Sitting up in her hospice bed surrounded by strange faces, loading invisible yarn onto an invisible spool, she let the motion wash her, keeping her away from thoughts of bedpans and who these people standing by her bedside were. I wonder what my motion will be. I hope it's not snipping.

The factory my mother worked in was a massive brick building with a thousand windows that had light blue paint over the glass, ensuring that nobody could see in or out. Just a blue glow from inside at night. When we'd drive by I'd imagine her inside the glow, hot glue and rubber tearing her small, tough hands. There had to be a way to get her out.

Money wouldn't be an issue soon. Once they saw my juggling credentials, which I wrote on the back of the psychosexual question page, they would send for me. Also included was a stack of pictures of me clowning, a bit show-offy, but they needed to see that I wasn't some junkie with nothing going for me. The one of me rolling out the barrel should cinch the whole thing with a belt.

After ringing the Pagans' doorbell and saying my goodbyes and fuck yous, I walked to the bus station carrying a stick over my shoulder, with a red bandana tied in a bundle at the end of the stick. Inside were cigarette butts and matches, a few shirts, juggling balls and a sandwich with some Chips Ahoy. I waited around the station until a driver finally noticed me.

"Joining the circus, son?" He looked like Wilford Brimley, concerned and gentle. He recognized the jester in my stare. When we locked eyes, his hooded lids assured me that Wilford was a comrade. He would put me on his bus and take me away to Clown College.

"Yes, sir, the circus! They're expecting me at the Ringling Bros. and Barnum & Bailey Clown College but my mom won't drive me. I have ten dollars from the clown shows I do. Is that enough to get me to there?" I was walking towards his bus as I talked, pointing at the map on the catalog, knowing he would tell me to hop on.

"What's your name, son?" said Wilford. I knew this line of questioning, where "What's yer name?" comes before "What's your phone number?" Soon he would want to call my mother and send me back. He was no friend to a dreaming clown. He was a traitor who wanted nothing more than to see me end up in some factory. Or the priesthood.

"What's yer phone number, son?" The bristles of his moustache lifted to reveal filthy teeth. The next question in this series is always "Where do yer folks live?" so I took off before he could say another word, hoping he wouldn't call the pigs. My sister once told me, as she puffed out the end of a joint, that all cops are pigs and I knew she was right. Wilford Brimley was a pig, too, I decided, as are all bus drivers.

In the rearview mirror of an abandoned station wagon, I painted on full clown face with the lotion and powder kit in my pouch, then headed downtown hoping to find my benefactor. Juggling three perfectly weighted rocks, I entertained the checkbook-balancing audience filtering in and out of the bank. If onlookers took notice of my evident gift, I would tell them "I can juggle four, you know," baiting them to ask me to show them, and getting me the big payoff. Most of them just smiled and continued on with the tedium of their lunch breaks; some of them put spare change on the ground by my pouch, mistaking me for a common street clown. Not one person asked me to do four. They were all pigs, I would later tell my sister, every last one of them. I put one foot in front of the other, in exaggerated clown steps, and marched up the street.

Dinner was cold when I got home. Boiled beef and carrots. I got a can of sardines out of the cabinet and fed them to the cat. We sat outside and waited for the sun to go down, me and the cat and a can full of fish. Nine months later, my pouch stank of soured Miracle Whip and cigarette butts. It sat in the corner of my closet, the stick-and-bandana looking authentic at last, with food stains and holes big enough for dreams to fall from.

They could at least have sent a letter.

I was born early, as in premature, one of those miracle babies so cherished in Roman Catholic families. *Oh, he's a miracle baby. Wasn't supposed to make it, ya know.* I was born jaundiced and cold to the touch, with an old-timey condition called The Rh Factor, which sounds like a teevee show but it's a real thing. There was a war going on inside my blood, I was rejecting it, allergic. I was immediately rushed to a larger hospital for a transfusion. Nervous hands passed me away and out of the hospital, away from my mother.

One hour old, needles were already penetrating my tiny veins, screaming. Bad blood out; good blood in. Some vibrating machine behind my head with its electronic *brrt brrt brrt*, pumping someone else's blood into my right arm as my own poison blood was sucked away. I wonder what they do with it, the poison blood.

This girl, April, who lived two houses down from the Pagans was born with it too, the poison blood. She was older than me and the science wasn't up to snuff when she was born so she didn't get the transfusion in time, and as a result she was retarded. That's what we said then. Mental retardation. April was retarded in a very profound way. She lived with her parents, a five-year-old brain trapped in a 22-year-old body. That could have been me, I thought. What would I be like? Would I stand around watching my posters for hours like I was looking out a window? Never go to school, drive, or live what everyone thought was a normal life?

My sister reminded me of my connection to April as often as possible. "Shut up, you were almost retarded," she'd say. "Retard."

"I am not retarded!"

"You are, too! Just not all the way like April. Ask Mom. You're a little bit retarded."

Maybe I was a little bit retarded and that's why I felt this way all the time, prickly and anxious. Sometimes I envied April and wished the transfusion hadn't come in time. We sat behind her one time in church as my parents were schmoozing their way to the front, row by row. Nobody wants to be seen in the back of the church. Or nobody can be seen, rather.

My parents sidled up, sixth row, sliding in behind April's family, my mother trying to get a good view, peeking around April's big hat. She had on her big hat and a fur coat, she was always so fancy. Even in summer she liked to wear her church coat, she said. I couldn't take my eyes off her. My mother wanted to rip her hat off so she could see Father Moe.

After communion — where the people line up, eat the host and take their sip of wine — we knelt at our seats, back in the sixth row. After it was decided we could sit and not kneel, a time frame I have never figured out, we sat. Small throat-clearing noises started from under April's giant muffin hat. It sounded like a bubble in her throat, some sort of trapped burp.

Wishing she would be okay, I looked up as she started coughing, a real gagging sound gurgling in her throat. I became transfixed, gripping the rail of the pew with my summer arms. The wetness pushing up from her throat brought the final hack, a plop of the chewed-up host, the Body of Christ, regurgitated onto the shoulder fluff of her rabbit fur coat. It just sat there, white cracker chewed and glistening, while my fingers pressed into each other, waves of empathy ripping through my tightened skin. I closed my eyes, hoping it would disappear from her jacket, the hunk of Flesh gelled in morning spittle, shimmying soft on the needles of a rabbit's fur.

In the early 1970s, my parents looked to take their faith in radical new directions. The search didn't lead in any fun directions, like

Transcendental Meditation or Satanism, but was more of an inside-the-box approach, like How Can We Get A Fire Under This Kettle O'Christ?

My family began its escape from the stoic practices of the Church by befriending the Bilders, whom my sister and I had always watched in wonder. My mother had been sizing them up for a few weeks by now, edging closer each time, pew by pew, until contact was made after communion during the Peace Be With You / And Also With You. The elite church people love this part of the mass. The who-knows-who part.

My mother reached around a second-pew person to shove her hand into that of Alice Bilder. "Peace be with you!"

"And al-so with you!" shouted Alice. Wilton was shaking my dad's hand right off the wrist, deliberate over-firm handshakes all around. The Bilders were the people that sat in the Front Row. Every church has them.

Wilton and Alice were the power couple at our church, boasting six beautiful children — three boys, three girls — all factually perfect. Wilton, with his lumberjack's build and silver hair, the same silver hair that coated his forearms and chest, stood like a tribute to virility, holding his huge arms high in the air as he prayed. He was the JFK Jr. of our Church, everyone wanted to be near him. His voice boomed the Apostles' Creed like nobody's business, loud and in charge, enunciating "We believe in One God, The Father, The Allll-mighty, maker of Heaven and Earth," on and on. It's a long prayer.

Every week, more eyes were on Wilton than were on the priest, who sat glowering from behind the wooden pulpit. Wilton made the pulpit for the church out of rosewood, sawing away shirtless in his driveway. Wilton was a real dick.

Alice Bilder, Wilton's wife, worked a puritanical blue twin set with black flats, a crinkly blouse choking her at the neck with a tight crucifix crushing the collar. Her ginger curls were a bit too tight, never brushed out enough, forming a round puff of dirty-penny crunch around her skull. I wanted to grab the hairbrush that my sister kept in her back pocket and go to town on Alice's head. Everybody wanted to.

My family started hanging out at the Bilders a lot. They lived in a two story/one-family country house on the corner. White, with white shutters, it was huge with a backyard barn and double garage. A compound, cut off from the street by a seven-foot white picket fence. A cartoon of a fence, it looked so tall to me as a kid. The slats were too close together so it seemed like a solid fence when you played inside it.

Wilton was forming a new group, a group of Church Families Who Sat in the Front (there were seven in all), who wanted something more. Saint Agatha's is a great church, Wilton said, but more was happening. He wanted to connect outside of church, to grow as families and foster ideas, to celebrate the Lord with abandon, unrestricted by the confines of a Sunday Mass.

Seduced by the strumming hands of the Hippie Jesus Movement, my parents traded in their rosaries for a tambourine and a belt-making kit. Copper buckles were shined and attached with rivets, holes were punched and within days all of us sported wide leather belts that said "Jesus Loves You" or "Jesus Is Lord" in block script, the individual letters burned in with an alphabet of branding irons by Wilton and The hideous Men. It was settled: we were in a cult.

The blood hit my sneakers in crimson hailstorm, loud plops of clotted tissue smacking down like hot cherry cordials onto the white leather of my new Nike Cortez. Joshua Bilder's friend stood in front of me yelping, a coat hanger stuck up his left nostril. All the way up and hooked onto the other side.

The taste of copper wire and blood filled his stomach as the Adults converged in a tight circle, throwing their hands and bodies onto him. The Men bound his arms from pulling at the coat hanger, keeping him from reacting, pulling down hard and making everything worse.

The women prayed. That's what they did, The Community. They prayed. Prayed as they removed the bent hanger from the boy's nose. Prayed as they ripped the wire out, leaving shredded sinuses and bloody nasal passages in its jagged metal wake. The Adults spoke in unknown languages, praying and mopping up blood as the boy's mother spun panic circles at the perimeter of the bloodbath.

Lu was the resident Church Lez at Saint Agatha's. Deep lez, complete with shag and Wranglers bearing the biggest key ring in New England, she was official. Nothing could pull Lu from her closet. "Satan, get behind this child! Remove the hanger and leave the boy... in Je-sus name, in Je-sus name, in Je-sus name..." she said, her voice joining the other peons, forming a choir chanting demands on The Lord.

Part exorcism, part medical emergency, the chanting ritual in the driveway pulled gawkers out onto their front porches, front row seats to the show. The Bilders always performed their Holy Acts as close to the street as possible. Wilton explained that exhibiting the miracles of Christ publicly, as Christ himself did, would draw more followers to the Community.

Shocked by the penitence of the Bilders and their small camp of followers, the neighbors gossiped, sometimes calling police when things got too bloody. When they could hear the snap of a whip coming from the garage, or the scream of demons escaping as finishing nails were driven in with a hammer, what else could they do but call 9-1-1?

The blood flow unstoppable despite several attempts at healing through The Power of The Lord, the boy's mother's instinct kicked in hard and she loaded her son into the back of her Volkswagen Rabbit to take him to the emergency room. Stitches, antibiotics, and a saline nasal spray to flush out the blood clots hourly.

The Community surrounded the car like zombies as she rolled up her window, her hand not turning the crank fast enough before they could cram their dead white fingers through the crack. She screeched off and never came back.

The Bilders lived close to my family. Two, three houses up on the right. I walked home alone, confused and wondering if the boy would die and what would become of me should I ever jam a wire hanger up my nose. Would I have enough faith to make it through? I doubted it.

I saw the kid at school the next week. He was in first grade, I was in fourth. Passing in the cafeteria, I'd crane my neck searching for visible scarring from the hanger but there was nothing. Wow, kids are resilient, I thought. Having heard it said about me so many times I knew it to be true. *If you woulda been one inch closer to the corner of that table you'd be dead. Dead.* Since there was no disfigurement I figured the kid was alright in the end. No prosthetic nose or difficulty breathing, at least none that I could pick up on when I passed. I counted the cracks in the sidewalk with a stick, vowing to never try anything with a hanger. My head was held low with thoughts of the boy as I walked up the stairs to the screen door. I didn't see her till I was on top of her and I backed up fast.

"This your cat?" A sixth-grader was standing on my front steps, holding a heap of teeth and blood clots matted in fur. Tigger's tag and blue collar were in the street.

The girl stared off, Tigger flattened dead in her arms. She was a big girl, tall and boney, and she clearly had a reputation, snapping her chewing gum the way she did. They must've held her back a grade or two; she was an absolute monster of a sixth-grader.

Her mom's car tire had Tigger's head pretty well smashed, almost to the point of full decapitation, but the girl kept holding on to him, her meaty hands waiting for some exchange, some impossible reward for the return of a mutilated cat. My mom took Tigger out of the girl's arms and said, "Thanks, hon," pretending she just received a box of Thin Mints and not a dead cat.

The killer was sitting in the car smoking, pretending she didn't just murder my cat. As for the girl, she wasn't moving from the top step. She blocked my exit with an I Could Kick The Shit Out Of You Right Now facial expression, like someone who'd been blocking exits their whole life. She was about to get real tough with me until wails of mourning launched from the back of the house. My sister, an eighth-grader, let the early stages of grief rip as my mom got the shovel out of the shed.

"Mom says Wilton said that you get your rewards in heaven so you better beat it. Especially before my sister gets out here," I told her. "If my mom comes back she'll try to make you go to church, you and your mother. You been baptized?"

"Of course I got baptized, stupid." She was getting nervous as my sister's screams got louder. "My whole family's real religious, we all got baptized."

"By fire? Your family been baptized that way? Feel the Holy Ghost all up on ya?" I sneered like a preacher, holding for a short pause, then ripped into her, "Or are you a sidewinder?" I stretched out that last word, raising my pitch for effect, aping the Men I had seen at churches and conventions.

The word I meant to use was *backslider*, not *sidewinder*, but it worked just the same. The girl didn't know the jargon any better than I did. I smiled at her as she spit her gum onto the top step, turned and walked back to her mom's car.

"Jesus loves you!" I screamed at the window of the car, a thick green Riviera with a low idle. They must have been new in town or they wouldn't have approached our house in the first place, dead cat or no dead cat. There were seven houses in our neighborhood whose families belonged to The Community, and we lived in one of the seven.

Kids would dare each other to ring our bell and run, like Jem and Scout did to Dill in *To Kill a Mockingbird*. Our house was the Radley house, a family of five Boos, but this is not a racial story. We were The People in The Cult, and most folks assumed that my mom would try and recruit them if they got too close to our house.

"Jesus looooves you!" I hollered again as the car windows went up and the killers rolled away. I didn't believe it but I screamed it anyway. Religious outbursts always seem to shut people up, and that's all I cared about. I'd seen it work before. My mother invited Jehovah's Witnesses into our house once and they never came back again. I don't know what she said but they wouldn't knock on our door again if they were burning to death, which, according to Wilton, was their inevitable destiny anyway.

After the incidents of the afternoon, and despite — or perhaps due to — my dispassion over the death of Tigger, my mother decided best I should stay home from school the next day. I agreed it was crucial that I took the day off, particularly with the big event slated for that evening. For this year, it seemed, I had found a way out of going to school on Halloween.

Halloween day isn't a whole lot of fun when you're the only cult member in your class. Every minute of every day all I wanted to do was dress up, Halloween or not. But Halloween could be the one day I wouldn't get laughed at for dressing up as Ruth Buzzi from *Laugh-In* with the big handbag. As I looked through my wig box, the resentment grew. I chickened out again and I never would find out if they would have laughed at me or not.

In an incredible mixed message, I was allowed by my mother to have wigs, props, and clown costumes of all kinds. She didn't love the idea but she didn't want to stifle me either. On Halloween, however, costumes from the wig box were not to be worn. Halloween was the Devil's holiday, and to celebrate it customarily was to do the Devil a favor, give him an inlet to pour wickedness into the souls of innocent children.

Halloween day the previous year I begged my mother to make me a costume like all of the other kids at school were wearing. I knew from past experience that all of the other kids would be dressed in elaborate costumes. Jessica would be a witch, Billy would be a vampire, and Tonya would probably be a kitty cat. Going to school out of costume, being forced to explain why I wasn't allowed to celebrate the holiday like everyone else, would be suicide.

I wept until my mother gave in and made me a last minute costume. She took a paper grocery bag and cut out two holes for eyes. She drew on a smile, put the bag on my head, and sent me off to school. The bag said *You have a FRIEND at Almacs* across the back in red letters. The eyeholes were too low so I had to keep pushing the bag up from the bottom. The kid with the killer *Magilla Gorilla* costume kept laughing and asking me what I was supposed to be but I had no idea, no answer. I kept that bag on my head all day.

When I got home from school I went about my usual routine of putting on clown make-up, getting a plate of Chips Ahoy and a big glass of milk, and settling in to watch *General Hospital*. God, why can't I live in Port Charles? Even Luke and Laura had costumes on. Shit, even

Edward Quartermaine was donning a set of fake-schnozz glasses. What about me? I grew intensely bitter as Bobbie Spencer walked into the hospital with bunny ears and a rubber nose on.

Dinner at my house was at four-thirty like clockwork. I washed off the clown lotion and Maybelline eyeliner, and assembled at the dinner table with my family. After we held hands and said grace, I spoke my mind. I told them how embarrassing it was, wanting them to realize how hurtful it was. Wanting them to make it up to me somehow, me explaining how I went to school as The Bag-Headed Boy, but they didn't care. They laughed.

They all nearly choked on their shepherd's pie, laughing. Laughing at me harder than Magilla Gorilla. Laughing as I ran from the table into my room, crying and punching my pillow. Laughing as I screamed, "I hate you!" at the top of my lungs. But it wasn't them I hated. It was Wilton who I hated. Wilton was making me hate my family. Wilton was making me hate God.

In lieu of allowing us to go trick-or-treating like the Normals, Wilton approved a Community celebration called the Light of the World Party. Held in the church basement, the party ran simultaneously with a meeting of Alcoholics Anonymous, draining all the anonymity from their group. By Monday, everybody at school would know that Mr. Demrest, the gym teacher, was a teetotaler.

For the party all Community members were required to wear costumes of a biblical nature, and Wilton called Jesus first. The Risen Christ version, with long flowing white robes and sandals. He jumped in with the alcoholics when they joined hands in their circle, leading them in the Lord's Prayer. Standing in costume with the drunks, Wilton was radiant, holding the hands of his partners way too tight and speaking in tongues. So happy to have them surrounding him, he played out the Gospel story of Christ and the lepers, trying to fix broken hearts and shaking limbs with what sounded like Pig Latin.

If they didn't want a drink before Wilton crashed their circle, they sure as hell would need one now. Even AA considered The Community to be a cult, so we must've been pretty official. The AA's quickly finished up their serenity prayer and got their wagon out of the church before our party hit full stride.

Apple-bobbing, Pin the Tail on the Donkey, and other church-friendly games were played for prizes. First place was a Bible, second place a plastic rosary and on down from there to fourteenth place. It was the Everybody is a Winner model of competition even for me, always ending up with a box of raisins. There were dangerous three-legged races involving dispassionate cult kids strapped together with leather belts, hopping through lanes of metal tables and fold-up church chairs painted brown. As the races went on, blood and prayer were as inevitable as the clotting of raisins when they set, sweating, in their box for too long.

Out the window I could see my neighbors, the Pagans, going door to door with impressive caches of razor-filled candies. Jennifer was dressed as a bumblebee and her brother Marty was a giant can of Raid. So clever.

I could imagine Marty bustling around before trick-or-treat, up and down the carpeted stairs, the final touches on his bug-spray costume being applied with splendid precision, while next door my mother dressed me as Nameless Shepherd. I looked like an eight-year-old oil magnate, wearing a blue and white checked turban that my father brought from the Holy Land, and draped in a yellow sheet, with sandals.

All I wanted was trick-or-treat, to take my chances on razor blades instead of listening to Wilton pontificate over the hum of The Community Music Ministry, singing away and strumming hard with thick picks. Some of them clicked tambourines, Lu dragged a stick down a corrugated, hand-held wooden Jesus fish, making a *krrrrr-it* sound in time with the honking band.

Running away to the Pagans was just a matter of disappearing after dinner, I thought. I spent a lot of time there, doing sleepovers whenever I could. My parents were so absorbed in The Community they couldn't attend the goings-on in their own nuclear family. I was free to do as I pleased, as long as I didn't bother them during Community meetings or work, which was most of the time, so I could do Ruth Buzzi unsupervised in the wall mirror for hours.

My father permitted us to live our lives as normally as possible when inside his walls. In exchange for robbing us of our childhoods he turned double agent. Holding the façade of a strict disciplinarian when in the presence of the misogynist Men of The Community, at home he stuck to the ideals of a working stiff, trying his best to give his family what they needed without interference from Wilton Bilder.

In the presence of Community members, mentioning the allowance of toys and props I had accumulated in my father's house was forbidden. No mention of the make-up and wigs cluttering my toy box, and sundresses and heels just one room over in my sister's closet, where I played *Normal City Girl*, a serialized performance piece inspired by Marlo Thomas in the teevee show *That Girl*.

Further mastering the mixed message, my parents forced us to give up our favorite rock group, KISS, for Lent. All the Christian organizations were focusing on the evils of KISS, claiming the name was an anagram for "Kids In Satan's Service" and warning parents about the backward masking on the records. From a book titled "Backward Masking: Unmasked," my mother learned that all rock groups, even The Captain and Tennille, were Satanists. So we gave up Satan for Lent.

We did it, too, we gave up KISS. Driving in the car my oldest sister would change the station when "Rocket Ride" came on the radio. We would plead from the back seat to cheat and listen to the new KISS song, *just the one song?* But my sister was a rock. Now that she had her license it was her responsibility to protect my father's car from accidents, spilled drinks and, during the Lenten season, Satan.

She wouldn't have listened even if she was alone. She was a Peter Criss fan, on the mellow, low end of the KISS fanaticism scale; I was rabid for KISS, especially Ace Frehley, with his toxic silver make-up and shoes I would've killed a nun for. My other sister claimed Gene Simmons as her favorite. Poseur. Though I loved Ace and his total look, I was *in love* with the hirsute Paul Stanley, something I was crystal clear with. All through Lent I was a kid without KISS, forcing me to find other costumes. No pointy make-up, no heels, nothing. No KISS. It was an eternity.

When the Satan-free Lenten season ended on Easter Sunday, each of our baskets held not only candy but a copy of the record albums *Hotter Than Hell*, *Rock and Roll Over*, and the much awaited *KISS: ALIVE II*. My parents were good people. Brainwashed, but good. They wanted us to have fun and we did. There was always love, not the constant tension floating in the air down the street at The Bilder compound.

My father saw the unhappiness the cult caused and even though the cult didn't pay his mortgage, he tried to make light of it, always entertaining the kids. He went along with my mother's religious whims often, attending giant Charismatic Christian conferences at the Providence Civic Center, as if being dragged to church on Sunday wasn't bad enough. When theology crimps my free time, you can keep it.

Twice a year we would drive to the big city and file into the venue under the cover of daylight. The conferences were always slotted for Saturday and Sunday afternoons, ruining any chance of weekend plans at the Pagans. Ten thousand Wilton Bilders from all over New England would take their seats, teeth shining white and unholy in the blast of the house lights, which would remain on throughout the length of the conference.

My dad kept me close by, trying to make me laugh, trying to undo any psychological damage that was being done. Always aware of my terrific sensitivity, my father held my hand as the Christian band began to play and the energy in the room turned claustrophobic, people already sweating, fanning themselves with anti-abortion leaflets. My father was no less terrified than I. The tension in my hand was digging into his with a force he didn't know I had.

"Is it that bad?" he said.

"Yes," I said, grabbing his wrist with my free hand.

The feeling inside the Civic Center would freeze me up. We'd go to the snack bar as much as possible, my dad buying me a Coke and him a beer each time. He wasn't the only one drinking beer. There was a line of people secretly drinking beer out of soda cups, some of them at a conference for the very first time and in need of brain lubrication to ease the confusion, some of them at a conference for the very last time, scarred and burned with no eyelashes and no remaining hope for healing. Some were just plain alcoholics trying to level out the shakes, and I was glad every time my father raised his brow to say *You wanna go back to the snack bar?*

Watching the Civic Center employees flitting around, refilling soda and beer kegs, sweeping up leaflets, we would drink slowly from our cups, my sneakers scraping against the red velvet carpet in the lobby, doing anything to avoid reentering the inner sanctum.

Through the curtain were thousands of people speaking in tongues, arms raised high to the metal ceiling. Kathryn Kurden pranced around the stage like Vegas royalty, laying her pampered hands on cripples in wheelchairs or with canes, knocking them backward with the Holy Smack of Jesus. People would shriek, falling over in convulsions, being slain in the spirit and cleansed of their sins.

All of this healing only made me think of horror and death. Why couldn't I feel the spirit that these people seemed to be so overwhelmed by? Why was I not being healed? There must be something wrong with me. These people were not faking it. They were feeling something, something powerful and spastic. Whatever it was, it was turning their lives over on to their ends while my life stayed the same.

The folks in the cheap seats were falling out, sweating, dancing. They were picking up on this energy that I couldn't feel. All I knew was I wasn't being healed. I couldn't be. I didn't feel anything. None of what made these people cry out in tongues or writhe on the ground ever got around to me.

At Wilton's prodding, while my father had run to the bathroom, I was dragged up onto the stage to face the healer, Kathryn Kurden. She floated like a ghost in her beaded turquoise gown and the bubble of light around her was thin and dark with gold flecks spinning everywhere. When I'd try to pin down a fleck it would jump to her ankles. She was mercury. Her hair was teased to the sky, poking out of her bubble. It must have taken hours. Only a corpse could sit through that much back-combing.

In front of the thousands assembled, her shaking hand reached out to my head, my bubble resisting hers. The force had her hand bent back when she pushed on it, pushed on my head. Pushing, pushing, her eyes blackening. I should be falling over and shaking, she knew that. She kept pushing, her mouth twisted and spiraling at the corners.

This healer woman had me convinced that I was dying, right there on the stage. *What am I being healed of? Is it curable? Is it my brain? It is, isn't it?* No saving this one, she thought. This is the damned, she thought, and I heard it. She knew I heard it and took a half-step. She thought she had easy game with a young kid but I couldn't feel her, I wouldn't feel her, and she hated me for it. Push. *It must be from birth, what I have.* Push. *Genetic.* I knew what she was thinking. She couldn't get me out of her head. PUSH.PUSH.PUSH. Did she know about me? How I was born allergic to my own blood?

I was pushed out, early and aware. The lights were bright; I couldn't see my mother. The tiny body of a tiny Christ dangled over my head by a tiny nail, and the plaster was cracking. I knew this crucifix could have fallen on my head at any moment, counting the seconds until it fell and impaled me, Feet-of-The-Savior-first, through the membrane covering the hole in my skull. Little baby Damocles, fighting against the prayers, one hour old. Fighting against the angels with their bright, smiling faces. Even now, smiling faces make me want to run and hide, to sink comfortably back into the cold concrete that created me.

On her next push I pushed back, and my bubble flashed as the sword dropped, she saw it all and fell back into the arms of her goons. People pointed and howled as Kathryn was fanned with missals. My father swooped me up and brought me up the aisle, past our seats and out to the lobby.

After the Revival, the faithful filed out of the Civic Center vibrating with the Light of Jesus, hooting like frat boys. Not wanting the magic to end, they cluttered the parking lot with lawn chairs and coolers full of Tab. Fish-shaped windsocks drooped from the antennas of wood-paneled station wagons, flopping limp in the windless Providence heat.

The lot was charged with the same carnival atmosphere exhibited at a Grateful Dead concert, and a passerby would be hard-pressed to tell the difference. The same long hair, acoustic guitars, incense, and copious hugging could be witnessed from a helicopter fly-over. I was convinced that the Charismatics were tripping their teeth out, all hopped up on Jesus. I wanted some but like any scene there was an elitist bent: if you didn't feel it, you didn't get it, and were thereby square. I lugged my tired little body into the back of my father's Impala and waited for the drive home, cat-napping to the entangled sounds of generators and The Saved speaking in tongues.

When I got home I knelt by my bed, recited the Lord's Prayer and said ten Hail Mary's. Something had to give. The Saints and the Angels were asked for their intercessions and I begged for a sign, some message that I could join the Saved. I tried to feel a tingle, a vibration dropping on my scalp like soft fingers, but nothing. My tongue tried to find the inspiration to blurt out foreign exclamations but all that would come out were the lyrics to "Sometimes When We Touch" by Dan Hill.

"Sometimes when We Touch" was one of the first 45s I bought when Lu drove us to Mammoth Mart one Saturday. I bought it thinking it would be dirty. When I got home and played it I realized it wasn't the disc of filth I had been hoping for. I pleaded with my sister to trade with me. She had bought "Strutter '78" by KISS. She did the trade. It is still the best deal I ever got. Somehow the lyrics stuck in my head when I tried to speak in tongues: *Sometimes when we touch / the honesty's too much / and I have to close my eyes / and hide.* It was as close to a foreign language as I could get. I felt ripped off again.

Does glossolalia just happen or do you have to practice? Everyone else seemed so good at it, each one having their own style of nonsense words at the ready. Wilton really had a flow. He would do a whole thing with his *shamanamama grrraamaaaalla luuuunti,* where it sounded like a combination of Nepalese and Latin, dished up from the depths of his throat. Very Churchy. I tried harder but the elusive "gift of tongues" was not in me. There was no way for me to access it.

I got into bed and lay there staring at the ceiling, watching its plaster dripping down in hardened points like the surface of the moon, Dan Hill swishing his lovey-dovey gibberish around my brain pan. *I wanna hold you till I die / till we both break down and cry...* My hands pressed against the sides of my head in hopes of dulling the mellow.

A few weeks after the last Conference, it was somehow decided that I should be able to attend my first concert, a trip with the boys, chaperoned by a van-driving neighbor. All the kids got to go, I said, and it was KISS, so. My sister was pissed. "Why does he get to gooooo?" I don't think she'd even seen Foreigner yet. *So* mad. She called me "hateful" in French. "Heeee gets to go?" She was pointing at me.

"Yuht, because he's going out with the guys," my mother said. She made these little ditch attempts, occasional one-offs to see if I wanted to hang out with the guys. Hunting trips, fishing, godforsaken ice races with stupid Boy Scouts. I forget what they called it. Something with Alpine in it, *Alpine Derby* or something, either way it was freezing, with stupid Boy Scouts competing, and obstacles and other things I hated. *Hunting.* Me with my dad posing in front of the woodstove — at five a.m., an hour I don't know unless I hadn't slept yet, even then — me looking evil and so pissed for being woken up I could kill a pheasant using my eyeballs.

KISS was not something I'd need to be dragged to. I was going. In fact, my mother would have to pry her own eye pencil out of my dead hands, and even then. I was already there, busy in my head planning my outfit. Nobody cared if it was a group of Satanists driving me. It was the '70s, in a Van. With the boys. I remember the ride, classic '70s from the movie in your head. Bubble windows, curtains. I shoved myself deep into the bowels of the Chevy Van and bounced on carpet, my sweatshirt getting snagged on the inside of the door. "Shit," I said.

"What?" said Marty.

"Whassamata, Frank?" said his dad.

"Nothing! I'm fine!" I ripped my sweatshirt from the door and sat up, they turned around and Marty's dad mumbled something. Probably about me. They all laughed. All I saw was my own bouncing.

The show was held at the Providence Civic Center, where just weeks before I watched Kathryn Kurden working her magic spells on the Charismatics. KISS was going to inhabit the same stage where my head got pushed. This time I wasn't dressed like a cult kid, in a bright orange shirt with a dove on it. Conversely, I had dressed up for the occasion. With my make-up and talcum powder flaking, I must have looked like a zombie Paul Stanley in Zips, but nobody cared. I fluffed my hair.

Past the red velvet curtains thick as doors, we took our seats. First row balcony, stage left, which was a certain drag for the Ace Frehley fan I was but still not too shabby. As soon as we settled, the boys and the rest of the room disappeared into a swirl of pot smoke, lighters — all those lighters — and the sound of people screaming WE WANT KISS WE WANT KISS like this mob, they were demanding it, all sweaty and swearing and openly puking into their fingers. I was enchanted.

My seat was the last thing I wanted at this tent revival and the lobby was a distant planet. I clung to the metal bar in front of me, waiting. Waiting for the voice. The house lights clacked off and the place went quiet for a second before going apeshit.

You Wanted The Best And You Got The Best: The Hottest Band In The World: KIIIIi-uuSSSS!

The demands were met. KISS appeared from under the stage, trap doors coughing with fog machines, their costumed bodies running back and forth in front of the sign. Oh, the sign, with its giant letters: *K-I-S-S-K-I-S-S-KISS-KISS-KISS-K-I-S-S* blinking in seizure patterns. Sometimes the lights would be all the way around the edges. Or one letter at a time. Or my favorite, the less common every light on the sign on, where the giant KISS would blind you for a second, blasting so much wattage that when you closed your eyes it still said KISS.

"Detroit Rock City" started and I fell over backwards. In 1978 there was zero regulation on how many explosives a band could have and KISS had a shitload of explosives. Giant flames on both sides of the stage licked the metal ceiling of the Civic Center, heating up my face.

"Hello!" screamed Paul Stanley, looking directly at me, pointing his right index at my face. Push. I needed a barf bag or a diaper, I couldn't tell. I was coming apart, shaking. The stage was going up and down mad with hydraulics, spirals of white light shooting out of Ace's guitar. And God of Thunder, with the blood? Oh my God, the blood!

Vibration shook my every cell in harmonic assimilation, synapses making connections that hadn't existed before the lights came on. People were falling out all around me and I realized, finally, I was on fire. Whatever it was the Charismatics had felt when Kathryn Kurden shuffled across the golden stage, I felt it now. I looked across the flames, and He looked right at me. It was God, in seven-inch leather heels, singing "Do You Love Me?"

"I do," I whispered, "I do," deep into the neck of my sweatshirt.

"Thank you!" he said to me. *Push.* My head rocked back on my neck. "Goodnight!" he shouted to the rest of the crowd.

The house lights came up to twenty thousand crazed teenagers in rubbed-off make-up. I was frozen by the scene, my new people, my new flock. Slow motion showed an eager girl sliding into a pool of puked-up Southern Comfort and Peach Schnapps, landing flat on her back while her asshole boyfriend laughed. She was running towards the front, hoping to be one of the groupies picked by the roadies to be taken backstage to *do it* with KISS. She probably would have gotten picked, too, she was so metal, but she never made it past the puddle, her cheap pumps snagging an undigested piece of filet o'fish that slid her legs out from under her. She jumped up, her perfectly big hair flattened to the back of her head, soaked with cold puke and warm Budweiser, the *drip drip drip* from the nest of her frizz pouring into the bowl of her cowl-neck sweater.

Nobody prayed over her, nobody called on the Infant Christ to heal her. Instead the entire balcony laughed, hoping another person would fall victim to the puke slick before security made them leave.

The parking lot was all blasting KISS, puke girl was laid out in the back of a tricked-out Mustang, and there wasn't a cop in sight and no Kumbaya. I rode this wave of Rock and Roll chaos all the way home in the Van, now knowing the truth: that I was good, I was part of something that I could feel. Driving home, I could still feel the heat of the flames from my spot in the cold van, and it still said KISS on my eyelids when I blinked. Marty's dad could kiss my ass for all I cared. I wasn't scared anymore. Every bump in the freeway made me rise up a little more and I knew I had been saved.

When I got home I was dazed, like I had aged ten years. I put on a record and went to sleep. Either the excitement or the healing was keeping me up. After the record was done it didn't pick up at the end, the needle repeating in the wide circle of grooves *ph-lup, ph-lup, ph-lup*. Sinking into the hum the skull makes when the ears are blocked, I pressed hard against my pillow. The hum began to morph into a whooshing, a new sound coming from outside my head, a sonic whoosh from the backyard. Not a whoosh like the wind, more of a backwards whoosh, like a vacuum.

Beyond the red shades that covered my window came a blink, then a solid light, like a streetlight coming on. Peeking through the side I saw a figure in my yard, floating a foot above the ground between the bulkhead and the shed. A swirl of flames with the outline of a body visible through the whiteness, the hands down at the side, palms out. The face on the body was that of Ted Neeley's in *Jesus Christ Superstar*, only it didn't sing or smash anything but just floated there, burning.

I couldn't break contact with the glass of my window, warm to the touch. The vision didn't say anything to soothe me; it was busy being a vision. My fear grew as it stretched out its arms, I wanted to shove my head down but I couldn't move. I had seen enough passion plays and movies to know what was coming next, with the nails. My throat closed up around my scream and I forced myself down, the surface of my bed shaking along with my body. I fell to sleep.

In the morning my red shades were still drawn, the sun behind them smacking filtered red light onto my walls like any other sunny day. The faces on my KISS wall posters hadn't changed. Paul Stanley was still beautiful, his one-starred eye telling me it was all a dream, like the UFO dreams and the Nuclear War ones.

Examining my hands for stigmata, I noticed half–moon shaped slices in the center of my palms, where the nails were driven. All oxygen left me as I waited for the holes to reopen and the blood to resume its flow. My nervous hands balled and I saw my fingernails slide perfectly into the grooves they had cut while I slept. Another mystery explained.

I wondered if all of the people who claimed to have received holy stigmata were only like me, stressed out to the point that their own fingernails ripped holes through their hands while they slept. There was no blood on the sheets, the impression of my fingernails fading as quickly as the memory of a dream. I rolled out of my waterbed and ate Count Chocula for breakfast which tasted the same with no holes in my hands (I tried to pour the milk through my palms, to be sure). I never told anyone about the emergence of the Risen Christ from the gypsy-moth laden lawn of my stolen childhood. Having visions didn't seem very Rock and Roll.

My sister wanted contact lenses more than I wanted Clown White. Going into ninth grade, she was as marked as I was. I can't imagine being a girl in ninth grade, let alone being The Girl in The Cult, the one with the big nose and glasses. My father felt bad for not being able to provide contact lenses, and for passing down the giant schnozz that they would bookend.

He saved up all his working-class nickels until he could afford the new eyeball covers she wanted. He was proud when she opened the package and saw them; I think we all cried. My family was always happy for one another when something went well. Not a lot of competition when the bar is so low. Not particularly encouraged, I never shot too high, something that is with me to this day.

When I wanted a paper route my mother said, "Oh, no way. I am not driving around in the rain at seven in the morning on Saturdays when you don't wanna wake up and do it. It's a big responsibility, Francis. You'll join up and then you won't do it, just like the Cub Scouts. Remember the Cub Scouts?"

When my sister got to remove her giant glasses, I was genuinely happy that she broke through to my parents. To her, they didn't say, "Oh, we'll get 'em for you even though you probably won't put them in." They just got them for her, knowing. And she wore them, too. Every day. Her old glasses sat on her cracked wooden shelf like a fossil; on one lens was a gold butterfly and on the other lens were her initials. They were that big.

When Wilton and the other Men in The Community found out

about the contacts, they called my parents into an emergency meeting with the parish priest, Father Moe. Moe was a raging queen who was later sent away from the Church — not because he was diddling boys but because he was having sex with men, and because they knew he was a big old 'mo. Father 'Mo.

"So, Wilton, what's this all about?" my father said.

"Maybe we should all sit," said Father 'Mo.

"Yes, maybe. Good idea, Moe," said Wilton.

My mom sat silent as Wilton took the seat across from my dad, took Father Mo's seat. Wilton was such a fucking donkey.

"We see you bought your Carlene some contact lenses... that's what we heard from the girls today, that Carlene had some contacts in at school."

"Yeah?" my father said.

"Well, we just don't think..."

My father's hands shook as he waited for Wilton to say it.

"...we just don't think you should be making such large purchases without consulting the Community first... or at least tell Moe here..."

"Father Moe," said Father 'Mo.

"Father Moe... sorry... but we — me and Moe — see this purchase as a reduction of your tithe, of our tithe, and we can't have that. You understand."

My father jumped out of his seat and held up his hand to the men with his middle finger extended. He never did it before, maybe once in the Navy, but giving the finger wasn't his long suit. Like me, when enraged, he turns into Don Knotts.

"Screw you, Wilton!" he screamed. "Screeew youuu!" His voice shook into the higher octaves, his register getting tighter with each word and his voice cracking. "I'll buy anything for my damn kids that I damn well want. You don't tell me how to spend my damn money, you big jerk!"

My father grabbed my mom and plucked her out of her seat — she was starting to cry — and pulled her out of the room, pushing past Wilton and through the door, walking out the clackety doors of the church rectory. "And screw you too, Moe!"

And that was it. As fast as we were in a cult, we were out. No deprogramming required. My parents got into their Impala and drove away.

"Well, that didn't go as well as I had hoped," said Wilton. "I guess some folks just can't be saved, huh, Moe?"

"Father Moe," said Father 'Mo.

I was pretty lucky that I never had to come out. It was already done for me, evidenced by my wig box and assorted props: cheerleading pom-poms, juggling bags, eye shadow sponges, and yarn. Nobody had to tell anybody anything. Trust: when your nine-year-old's "down time" fills itself with walking serpentinely through the house in a blonde bouffant wig and digging through your dresser for Maybelline eye pencils, you don't need to do the math. Equation solved. Marty Pagan's toy box lay in sharp contrast to mine. He had not an old wooden toy box but a new one in the shape of a giant NFL football, the smell of thick plastic surrounded it from a solid foot on each side. It had its own aura. This giant toxic football like an advertisement, stuffed with tennis balls, catcher's mitts, and the hand-held sports games that bugged me with their constant squawking for touchdowns or more batteries. Above the sports slush and the electronic games screaming feed me hung every baseball card ever printed, screwed to the wall on display.

Above my wig box — the wooden crate that was a tangle of synthetic hair — hung no such paraphernalia. Other than my KISS posters, I didn't hang much. There was a personalized letter from Leo Buscaglia, whom I'd written to after reading his book, *Love*. A picture of me with The King at a Medieval Times in Florida — the King just looked like a dude from Orlando, not particularly enraged by his job. I looked by far more uncomfortable in my Vacation Costume posing with a character actor in a theme restaurant.

Next to that was a picture of me posing with Willie Whistle, the local clown of my youth, at a senior citizens facility outside Boston. I have no idea how I even got there. Driving to Boston was always a hassle for my parents and we rarely did it. We barely even crossed into the Massachusetts border towns that surrounded us in fear of The Massholes, or as we called them, The Hillbillies. Rushing home from third grade to make sure I caught my stories — *General Hospital* was gearing up for the Ice Princess and big things were happening — I'd see the other kids planning their afternoons. Shooting hoops, skateboarding, and eventually, thank god, playing Atari. I sat myself in front of the full-length mirror in my mother's room. She was ironing, singing a Mama's and Papa's tune as I patty-caked against the mirror.

Having nobody to practice with, my stoned sister proving no help time after time, I depended upon myself to learn the hand-clapping routine. The order in which to clap, pat, cross your hands, or slap your knees was critical business in the schoolyard, at least among the circle of girls I watched at recess. I wanted in. As my only competition I got wicked fast real quick and before I knew it I was a blur of arms in front of the mirror.

…old lady mac, mac, mac

Marty Pagan was coming up the driveway, I could hear him dragging some piece of metal sports equipment. I knew he was going to bother me so I picked up the pace of my clapping, patting, and crossing, dropping the total hint. Ignorant, he came to my mom's window.

"Hey, do ya wanna come play baseball with us?"

…all dressed in black black black

"Shhhhhhh!" I said. Clearly, the rhyme wasn't over. He was bothering me in the middle.

…with silver buttons buttons buttons

"Hey, Francis, you wanna come play baseball?" he repeated. They must have needed someone bad. My concentration was broken and I was getting flustered.

"Can't you see I'm busy? What's wrong with you?" I said in the mirror, his stupid half-head in the window. I started my hand claps again, from the top.

…old lady mac, mac mac

"Why don't you wanna play baseball?" Marty was incredulous,

outside the window, standing on my baton with his stupid sneaker.

… allll dressed in black, black, black

I got louder. I wanted to take that bat to his head and really swing. He was bugging me now.

"And why are you always practicing those girl games?" he said.

… with silver buttons buttons buttons

Before I could jump up and run outside, my mother slammed her iron down onto its board, mashing the *steam on* button, leaving spurts of hot water and tea-kettle clouds blasting behind her as she marched to the window. Her little body could really move when she was pissed, and she looked like she was going to rip Marty in two.

"He's *good* at it. That's why he practices, Marty, because he's *good* at it… now move your feet outta here… do what *you're* good at and go play your baseball, you little shit."

… all down her back back back

Marty looked at my mom and ran away, schooled.

"He's a little shit," she said. "You're good at it. Keep going, hon…" My mother was free and happy outside of the cult, ready to pick battles and say "shit" outside the house.

She started singing again and my hands regained their speed, challenging their own reflection. My mom was right. I *was* good at it and I would patty-cake, satisfied, until I could move on to public transit and bigger towns.

Once I discovered RIPTA — the Rhode Island Public Transit Authority — my preteen life started to blossom. Able to going to the mall on my own schedule, I'd run from the entrance straight to the Waldenbooks across from the Deb shop.

Deb, with its bubble mirror façade, reflecting everything in front of it thousands of times. With headache lighting and belt racks, I couldn't stand going in there with my sisters. Deb smelled like thin leather and carpeting, and gave me an instant headache.

Waldenbooks soothed that headache with its folksy name and wooden shelves. The staff was lax, there was access to any kind of material, and it smelled like books. It still smelled like carpet, too, but not like Deb. Waldenbooks seemed so cozy back then, like a real smart person's book place. Mall regulars called it simply *Walden's*. Nobody had any ideas on Thoreau, preservationism, resistance, things like that, but they knew Walden was something literary. "Like Whit Walden or what's-his-name up Walden Woods, up in Mass… on Golden Pond or whatever," my dad told me when I asked.

The copy of *The Joy of Gay Sex* was hidden there at Waldens in the Politics and Finance section, where nobody ever went, not even the staff. I didn't hide it myself but I found it and kept it hid. There were probably six of us, all complete strangers, feeding off the secret of our communal hiding place. Looking at the book, I couldn't believe what I was in for. So lame. The drawings were so shitty they weren't even dirty. The sketch labeled "oral passive" was particularly boring, its curvy lines making me feel as if I had already done it before.

Deflated, I would go to Spencer Gifts and flip through the dirty poster display in the back, skipping past all the Cheryl Tiegs and the Cheryl Ladds and all the Cheryls, *swip, swip, swip,* the blacklight Boston poster, *swip, swip,* the acid-head poster, *swip,* the pot-leaf poster, *swip, swip, swip,* until I got to the hairy fireman one, where you could see the top of his bush poking above his yellow rubber pants with red suspenders.

I would stand gawking, thinking more about the red suspenders than oral passive, until a gaggle of teenagers — a demographic that works my nerves to this day — would come back to check out the strobe lights, lava lamps, and posters of the Cheryls.

Flipping to a Cheryl as soon as I heard their stupid cracky voices, I would hold it open, afraid they would know I was looking at suspender fireman. "'Ay, Sherrrrr-alll," they'd say as they passed the poster, like Damone in *Fast Times* with the Deborah Harry cut-out, all *oh… Debbie… hi…*

It was a magical world, the back of Spencer Gifts, and my time there was always ruined by some zit-faced asshole who wanted some fake dog shit or punk sticks or a Cheryl. Eventually, RIPTA would take me past the mall all the way to Providence where I'd find the smaller bookstores, with not only great books I'd never heard of, but entire rows of filth way better than the suspender fireman shit at Spencer's.

My bus pass lasted another year before I got my license, the giant Volvo tires of the RIPTA bus kneeling to the yellow curb with a hydraulic *pssssttt,* dropping me off to find the sleazy alleys and parking lots where I would at last come to understand "oral passive" in a very physical way. I even made a little lunch money.

I wasn't one of those kids who'd need to be prodded to get a license at sixteen and move out at seventeen. Providence laid over a hump in RI Route 146, its small skyline flickering with two windows of my first apartment.

My sublet was with some Goth kids from just over the Massa-chusetts border. They were real Goths, too. It was the late '80s so there was no trending, no #Goth. These were the kids who would later end up on *Jenny Jones* or *Sally Jessy Raphael* or some other daytime talk show, talking about piercings or hairdos or nightlife. They weren't talking in public about cutting yet, just the look. The Goth Look.

I didn't have the Goth look, or any look at all. Not that I didn't try. When I moved out of my mom's, my hair was past my shoulders and frizzy, beholding a brown that didn't have warmth or ash, just rat-fur brown. One week at the Goths had me deciding to tint it black. Jet Black was the color on the box. Instead of lending an edge to my look, Jet Black only washed me out, making me look even more like the hippie clown I already was. Better wigs could be found at the Salvation Army, outside the store, next to the big red box. Same with my clothes.

To remake myself in my new Big City Life, I called a hair salon to do something about my look. My mother paid. She'd always told me, "You cut that hair, Francis, and I'll pay. I don't care if it's fifty dollars." I phoned in the favor.

The salon was all brass and glass, called Glitz Iz Hair! It was the closest place to my house. When I walked in there was a dash for the back by all the available stylists. They poked their heads out one by one, each one assessing from afar whether I had bugs crawling in and out of the mass of black pill on my head.

"No way," they all said, until finally the owner had to come out. I wasn't leaving.

"Hi! Welcome to Glitz Iz Hair!"

"Oh… hi."

"I'm Krissy, the owner." She lifted her arms in a wide V and slowly lowered them in an Everything You See Here Is Mine sweep.

"Cool…" I looked around. I hadn't been in a whole lot of hair places and they all looked the same to me, only Glitz Iz Hair had more chairs than other places I'd been. All those empty chairs, someone would have to take me.

"How can we Glitz you up today?" Krissy was being hopeful. I was the last person that belonged at Glitz or in any place of beauty. I felt as foreign as she thought I did, looking around at the style books and expensive products.

"Well, I need a haircut…"

"Mmm-hmmm!" she said.

"And once it's short, I want it blue."

"Oh, yes!" She was now seeing me as a complete make-over, and make-overs were just hitting their stride. She threw herself headlong into the challenge. "I can see you in blue. Yuht. Totally."

I felt like Eliza Doolittle at the beginning of the story. "Okay, cool… I'm ready, Kristy."

"Krissy," she tapped at her nametag, "K and double s. Pah-pow." Pistol fingers.

"Gotcha… Krissy. I'm Francis."

The following hours were a blur of flying hair, sizzling bleach, and attempts at blue. Krissy was not giving in to my hints that it was fine without blue, that maybe red would be fine and that I couldn't sit anymore, that I wanted out of Glitz Iz Hair before the sun went down. I couldn't make her understand that I didn't care. My head was now her project and that was that. If she had to strap me down to do it, I'd wait until it was blue.

All the stylists were packing up for the day, smiling at me now that my hair pillow was gone, swept into the sealed bucket marked HAIR. They were amazed at my patience.

"I guess you gotta suffer for beauty," said her main stylist, some failed port-town leatherman with a pinched face and unfortunate facial hair.

"Really?" I said.

"Oh, yes… yes, girl. I mean look at me!" He spun, his bottom shoved into a pair of thin fashion-chaps over tight white denim. The look on top was a white pleather jacket and an open shirt exposing his chest acne. "This didn't happen without considerable suffering, honey."

"Yeah, we know," Krissy snorted. "He makes us suffer every day!" She was cracking up, oblivious to the lavender tone my hair was taking on, the way my hands were tightening around the arms of her chair.

"Whatever it takes, bitch!" said Pleatherman.

"Don't *bitch* me... bitch!" Great comeback by Krissy. I couldn't believe the way they talked to each other and couldn't imagine spending ten more minutes in this puffy modern chair.

"I think I'm gonna go. It's fine the way it is, Krissy. It's really, um..."

"Blue?"

"Well, not really blue, but close enough." I wasn't even convincing myself. It was pink in some spots, lavender in others, all pastels. No blue.

"Oh, it's blue," said Pleatherman, winking at Krissy over my head, forgetting about the mirrors. How can they deal with all the mirrors?

"It's just, like, a pinky-blue," she said, spinning me towards her. "Not a royal blue, but more of a pink-blue, right?"

Not sure who she was asking I answered, "Well, sure, but then that's not blue then, if it's got a special name like pinky-blue... but it's fine." I added, "I like it," squirming under the weight of shitty lies. Pinky-blue would do nothing to help me develop my own look, and with the precedent now set, nothing would. I wanted my frizzy hippie hair back from the can.

"Well, good! I'm glad you love it. I love it, too," said Krissy.

All this lying and changing around of word meanings was making my head hurt worse than the second bleaching. I paid at the desk with my mother's blank check, seventy dollars. I wrote it out for exactly that.

On the way back to the apartment I stopped at CVS and bought more Jet Black. Little kids were pointing at me, their mothers not stopping them. Seeing a brokedown queen with a pinky-blue clipper-cut in the Hair Care aisle is no time to begin tolerance training.

In the parking lot I mixed the ingredients, pouring bottle A into bottle B, and threw it on my new short hair and drove home while it processed, cursing Hair Salons and hoping nobody saw me leaving Glitz. My hair was better upon rinsing it out. Short and black. I could have done that, I thought. My hair looked fine. Now if only my clothes would fall into line.

The art student we subleased the apartment from, Mira, was a White-Clad Goth, which at the time showed enormous bravery and hinted at a bigger budget. She was a Fashion Student, so a white smock number with ripped tights and white vegan shoes wouldn't cut it. She was High White Goth, and even the then-emerging John Fluevog shoes were too ordinary for her. Everything was turned out. Her boots were pointed baby shoes, a matte talc color with three eyelets and a boutique name inside the tongue, some place in London.

Mira attended the Rhode Island School of Design and when she took off for summer break she'd left plastic bins of clothing under her bed. These were things she didn't want to schlep back and forth between semesters so I rationalized she didn't care for them much and began rifling through them as soon as I knew she was back at her parent's mansion in Dallas.

I wanted the entire experience of being Mira, of having an up-and-coming art career, a few interested boys, some pencils, and a Mission Statement. To absorb her artsy realness I'd lay on her futon in my underwear and run my fingers down the string of white Christmas lights, across the lip of her leather portfolio and up the side of an Art History textbook. Throwing on one of her original designs, a white V-neck t-shirt covered in a white mesh vest, I'd lay there pretending I had a style of my own, my short blackened hair wrapped with a ridiculous headband. Through proximity, if nothing else, I'd become the artist I wished I was, or at least work out the poses of having a direction.

Going on teevee daytime talk shows in the early '90s was something that paid to pose and, being so good at it, I did it whenever I could. As long as there was a check at the end I'd have said just about anything for two hundred dollars, a plane ticket, and a shitty room. My Goth housemates got way more action than me in the daytime trash teevee world but I was pulled along into the mix as the voice of reason, my lies and atrocious fashion sense setting the premise and tone for entire segments.

The first *Jenny Jones* was the best. Like anything else that's fun, going on teevee became less and less fun each time. No matter how hard I'd try to recapture the initial excitement, it would never be as electrifying as that first visit. Ours is an incurable, progressive, and often fatal disease.

Chicago. Who knew it would be so cold I'd beg for Maine? Unable to pack for the weather, I always carry the equivalent of a jean shorts and fannypack to any place outside of New England. The foolish pride of growing up with tough winters reveals itself when you're the only one risking hypothermia at an art installation or wearing a tank-top to Chicago for the taping of *Jenny Jones*. There wasn't always Google and the Weather Channel cost money. I didn't have a ham radio so all I brought was the green shirt.

I wore the green shirt on every show; it's how I recognize myself in reruns. I borrowed the shirt from my cousin who was twice my size. It had white buttons and a wide collar. The color wasn't the electric green of my psychic shield but a mortal green, more moss than gloss. It, combined with whatever horrid pants the show insisted I throw on, would swallow me up with its enormity and I reverted to a Muppet, shrinking into the bulk of my borrowed outfit as soon as the red applause sign lit up.

The first episode, "You're Having a Bad Hair Day," centered around Liz, with her hair up to there, tinted navy-blue/black and shaved on the sides. Liz was beautiful, even without the hair. But the hair didn't hurt; it took a ton of work and paid off double-time. It was amazing that people at the studio thought it looked bad. Duly amazing was that a loser like me also thought it looked bad, and would go on a talk show to process. I wouldn't just say it, I'd say it on teevee. I'm gonna be famous.

That first show went easy. Liz erupted, as she was instructed to, when I said her hair looked like shit, repeating the words in the same tenor the producer had told me to. It hurt my teeth to say it in practice: "You're having a bad hair day, every day," but once those hot lights were on and there were morons clapping I would have screamed in the face an incubated infant for more air time.

In the green room there were always people competing for longer segments, comparing notes before the taping.

"Our daughter has cancer."

"Yeah, well, my roommate has some ridiculous hair, so, excuse me..."

"She's twelve," they'd say, insistent that it was me who gave their daughter the cancer.

"I'm sorry," I'd say, pushing them out of the way to get to hair and make-up. "Twelve. Well, that sucks. She's cute, though! Cute is good! Have fun!" I was not above roughhousing. "Now, excuse me," I'd say, with a shoulder push to Dad and a wink at cancer girl. "Make sure you get the check, doll."

It was fun whether they liked it or not. There were people on set whose job was to use giant make-up puffs, hand-sized clouds of clean cotton or synthetic that packed my pores with the life-giving blessing of pancake make-up. What's not to like? I was hooked.

We didn't get a double-segment. Me and Liz weren't that great the first time. We kept laughing at each other. We had all these ridiculous lines planned out and would crack up when they were spoken out loud in front of the audience.

"Just because I'm subversive doesn't mean I'm unimportant," said Liz, using her favorite line and causing me to buckle into my laugh, the guy getting pissed and waving his arm like CUT as they had to stop rolling again.

"CUT!"

We were wasting a lot of time, and it turns out that cancer is a real tearjerker. Jenny loved tears, so we got beat. Next time.

I wasn't going out like that, losing my future to some weepy Midwestern family struggling with a terrible disease. As soon as we returned to Providence, I got on the horn. I put on the green shirt to make the call. Miguel's cousin gave us a lead on some show in Los Angeles, a city I had only dreamed of and wouldn't have otherwise made it to.

"Hi, I'm Francis, and my friend Liz, she's a girl... yuht... anyways, she has all this facial hair and I want her to shave it... yeah, she's a girl... it's really gross..." I couldn't believe what was coming out of my mouth. I loved Liz and, even more, I loved her facial hair. A clean little moustache and four scraggles of tight wires poking out of her chin. She was perfect.

"So she's hairy, is that it?" said the voice of the gatekeeper.

"Is that it? Whadda ya mean, is that it?"

"Well, I mean, does she dye it or comb it or anything? Or is it just there?"

"Oh, yeah. Oh, no, she combs it," I said, "all day long. She twists it around her fingers even."

"I see." Horrified pens began their scribbling. Female Facial Hair Proudness, today on *Walk Away!* They bought it hook, line, and sinker, and by week's end, Liz and I were on an American Airlines flight from Logan to LAX.

Walk Away! was a show that brought together people who had an irreconcilable rift and left it up to the host, who looked like John Tesh, to decide whether the issue could be hashed out or if they should Walk Away! and never speak again.

In the green room, Liz kept saying, "How are we doing this and feeling good about ourselves? You don't really hate my moustache, do you?"

"No, no, no, oh my god, no... I love your face. Just think of it as your face and my lies are paying the rent."

"I'm gonna shave it," she said, in earshot of the production assistants.

"No," I said. "Do not under any circumstance, no matter what I say, no matter how vicious I am, do not shave it."

By the end of our segment, out marched an intern with a Dixie cup of warm water, some Barbasol, and a disposable razor laid out on a room service tray. He shoved it at Liz, like here... now shave it.

I was mortified as Liz took the warm water and shaving cream, rubbing it onto her upper lip and chin. In the repeats, you can hear me mumbling under my breath, "Don't shave it. Leave the beard. Please leave the beard."

"I will," she said, finishing off her top lip. She left the beard.

"Thank you," I said, looking to the confused audience who had bought my green-shirted lies. They saw right through me. I saw right through me.

The check for that show didn't have the same heft as the first *Jenny* and, try and try again, my lies were weighing me down and cracking the buttons on my cousin's green shirt. These scripted talk shows were taking something back with every penny they paid, and I knew I'd have to get out eventually. I was sick of being the one that hated everyone's hair, like I could do any better.

Over time, different shows had me lie about other things besides hair: teen pregnancy, paternity, drug use. But I was only truly good at lying about was how much I hated people's hair.

The shows' writers would cast me as the judgmental friend or the boyfriend of a pregnant girl. They never did an "I'm Here, I'm Queer" episode using me — ignoring my possibilities — so viewers were expected to believe that I was capable of impregnating the girl next to me and then fighting about it, all because Ricki Lake seemed concerned. I don't see how it worked but it did, and somewhere in some basement there's a reel of me on various talk show couches, appearing as an effeminate hetero choad with six abandoned biracial children.

My daytime talk show career fizzled quick. There were only so many episodes you could go on before you'd covered all the bases, been hosted by all the hosts. Plus the people that watch those shows watched them all. They knew the guests and could spot a repeat player from the kitchen. The *Phil Donahue* crowd went straight into *Geraldo*, then *Jenny Jones*, *Sally Jessy Raphael*, and the lesser known *Rolanda Watts*, who was a godsend, paying $250 a lie. I think Rolanda was a doctor but everyone called her Ro, so maybe she was one of the cool doctors that were arriving to daytime teevee. My mom thought I would be famous.

"He's on teevee, my son… on teevee." Every time I called her she would ask, "Sooo… are youse on teevee this week? You really gotta keep up with it, it's not gonna just *happen*, Francis. Have you seen these other kids, with the polka-dot faces? More like that, Francis… dress it up…"

Nothing I could tell her would convince her otherwise. Nobody became famous from being on these shows unless they did something outrageous like chopping up a drug dealer and throwing the body into the Hudson. Not only did I not have the capacity, I didn't have the right shoes for that sort of thing. Clubland homicides require at least a ten-inch platform sneaker, and the clubs were in New York City.

We didn't have Club Kids in Rhode Island. Just the one weirdo bar where we all hung out, every night, no matter who was playing. Providence was special that way, hosting a true working-class anti-scene, where the labels that other places held fell away. With so many colleges in Providence it was us against them, college kids vs. locals.

Me and The Goths got on great in cohabitation. Most people here got along, a common thread of local pride running through the hippies, the punks, and the Communist Commune run by Fred the Red. While my mom bragged to her friends about my television fame, in Providence we were famous for nothing besides being the Townie creeps that fucked with the college kids. We were merciless, filling water balloons up with ketchup, vinegar, and turkey-baster chicken grease to huck at visiting parents and alumni of Brown and RISD. We'd run up and whip them right smack into the baldest forehead, spraying the people in line behind it with heinous combinations of condiments.

Assaulting Ivy League families was as fun as being on Ro but it didn't pay two hundred and fifty dollars and we all needed the money. For my rent money I would take odd jobs that promised nothing. I'd drive to a Massachusetts border town and work at a call center. One such place was TopQual and the people there called it TQ. Every day felt like a small adventure, traveling out of the safe space of Providence into hostile Masshole territory. TQ showed me what I had suspected going in: jobs like that are worse than poverty.

A headset was strapped to every head in the building, their cords plugged in to a hulking computer, an anchor keeping us in our seats. A swipe card measured my time, all very fancy technology at the time. TopQual was a hard job. The calls that came in were not the kind of calls anyone wants to get. It was the number to call for people whose camera film got lost or ruined during processing, so answering any line at TQ guaranteed an already irate customer on the other end, and there were lines of them, waiting, *blink blink blink.*

"Thank you for calling TopQual, this is Francis." Deep inhalation, eyelids tense.

"Don't *thank-you-for-calling* me, fuckhole! This is the third time I've called on this and my film from my honeymoon is still gone… just gone… like what'd ya do with it to make it gone, fuckhole? Is that your name, Fuckhole? That's yer name… Fuckhole… well, I'll sue yer ass… you watch."

While allowing time for the person to finish their rant, you'd type into the computer what was happening: *July 9th - Customer renamed me Fuckhole and has threatened a lawsuit. Still not sure what's going on.*

When there was a natural break in the cussing you could deliver your next line. "I'm really sorry, Mr… um, Mr. Herbert, is it?"

"You know goddam well who this is and don't tell me you're sorry, Fuckhole. Sorry. Sorry. Sorry, my ass! That's what I say! Sorry, my big fat ass. You hear me?"

"Yes, I hear you and can say that I truly am sorry. May I offer you three rolls of film on the house for your troubles?" Three rolls was always where you started, ten rolls being the maximum handout.

"Three rolls of film… oh, three rolls of film. Ya think they haven't tried that one yet? How about the roll you lost? How 'bout I just get that one back and call it a day?"

"Four rolls?"

"Fuck you, Fuckhole! Thanks for losing my memories!" *Click. Blink.*

People said that a lot, that I lost their memories. At the beginning I'd try to explain that I hadn't done anything at all and furthermore I was in no way responsible for their memories — lost film or no lost film — but there was never enough time. *Blink. Blink. Blink.*

"Thank you for calling TopQual, this is Francis."

This was my first exposure to Corporate Culture, surrounded by the company cheerleaders who listen in as you try to explain to someone how memories work. Some higher-up member of the corporate pep squad was always waving their arms at me from their offices, mouthing through the glass "Be nice!" They were always listening in, like having two people answering every call. I'm sure they did this for a reason, as damage control when an employee blows their stack after too many abusive name-changes and goes off on a customer. It happened once a week. High turnover at TQ.

A woman I shared a cubicle row with, Lurlene, jumped the banana wall one Easter, screaming into her headset, "I didn't do anything to your damn pictures, you bastard! And if I do find your stupid pictures I'm gonna burn 'em! Fuck you, too!" She stood. "And you and you and you ... fuck all of you!" She was pointing at all of us, shaking the cubicles hard, tiny wall decorations falling off of pushpins and puffing onto the carpet. Her headset was swaying from her plastic earring hoop, the forward momentum of her decision ripping the cord out of its place on the computer and following her out to the parking lot where security took it back.

We could see her howling as she sped off, both middle fingers in the air and steering with her knee. Total freedom. We all touched the glass as she disappeared, hoping to absorb some of the magic she left in the blowing gravel. I wanted to follow her but Lurlene had a plan. I had no other job offers except for RidCo, the place across from TQ. The folks at RidCo did "disaster cleaning," which often meant scrubbing blood and charred remains from linoleum floors after apartment fires or murder/suicides. Scratching at burnt skin with a painter's knife paid alarmingly less than TQ but it was starting to sound like an even trade.

Easter was the only Jesus holiday I spent at TopQual. Jim, the office manager, ran all around the office with pink bunny ears on passing out candy-filled plastic eggs screaming "HAPPY EASTER!" at the top of his lungs and ordering everyone to open their eggs. Normally I would be only mildly uncomfortable with someone's choice to put on a costume and force Christ's resurrection eggs on me but it wasn't a choice on Jim's part. They made him do it even though Jim was Jewish. A Jew in an Easter bunny costume. They asked him to do it and he did it. He passed out them eggs and screamed "HAPPY EASTER" with a smile on his face.

Jim does everything with a smile. He tells me not to be late again with a smile. He tells me *you can't get your check today* with a smile. Everything with the smiling.

The words "it takes more energy to frown than it does to smile" whirl around my head in a dialogue bubble. I knew all these things already from plastic-framed posters hanging in churches or institutions. The posters hanging around the walls of various places of salvation always seemed to start with smiling through it all. They should all say *Martyr Yourself*.

If you're really good at assimilating the cruelty of TopQual, you'll end up on the W.O.W. board, which stands for Winner of the Week. I know I won't be around long enough to be the Winner of the Week. I've never been the Winner of the Week. I already knew I liked quitting jobs better than I liked getting jobs. Never ever want to settle into some cubicle and give you two years of my life with my gums getting dry from all that easy phony smiling.

Jim tries to hand me a certificate that says *Good Job* on it, expecting me to jump up and down like he'd just handed me a diploma. If he only knew every night I would drive home wondering if I would go in the next day.

Over my short time in Providence, I'd developed quite the little heroin habit, and working TopQual was barely cutting it. The habit started at a party in one of Providence's more notorious lofts, a place I would eventually live in after I left The Goths, first as a tenant and later in the hallway. A few older Providence legends lived there, people who had broken other people's knees, carried bodies in their car trunks or sawed off one of their fingers while playing electronic music on a table saw. They were mythical. I'd hang out with them whenever I could, sitting amazed at their capacity for drug use. They did everything at the loft, no drug was off limits, and after two visits, heroin was placed in front of me. Powder, straight up the nose.

It was everything you've read about in books about drugs only not as richly written or lovingly remembered. It was all of it, every cliché: *love at first sight; my soul mate, heroin; it was fuzzy and warm and everything was right.* I started doing it a few weekends a month until I started buying my own and then it turned into all the time, just like that. I hid it from The Goths and everybody outside of the loft circle which can be easy when you're early on in the heroin relationship. It gets harder to hide as it progresses, when people's CD collections begin to get thinned out and gold rings aren't sitting in anyone's jewelry box where they were just yesterday.

Outside the small drug circle I had nobody to tell I was doing heroin, and since misery loves company, I had to find a little of both. I'd walk from the Goth house to the dancey gay bar, the one with the spinning lights and the cubes for people to dance on. You've totally been there. Sometimes I would get lucky and there'd be a cute face with a gaze and a few twenties for drinks and pilfering but more often than not I'd end up walking to the weirdo bar to sulk, hoping for another weirdo with heroin.

As the night crept to a close it would get more and more desperate, the misery settling in and becoming a beacon for worse and worse company. There were repeats of the same mistakes, going home more than once with the bandana guy who lived in his mom's basement or the sweaty guy with elephantitis of the testicles, twice. They were like softballs.

My first real boyfriend, Sudsy, was the worst person I could have been with. He was such a shitty running partner. In his time with me, he would go on to become most bush league heroin addict ever. He even called it *horse* once. The night we met he was pretty fucked up, we both were, as decided at the bar.

"My roommates will have some pot," I told him. Of course they would. The sweet Providence Goths, they're a special breed, different from even Boston Goths. Less showy, more factory.

When we got back to the apartment it was a full-blown happening. From the street it looked like nothing was going on but the dim living room entrance revealed mesh-covered bodies slung across couches, a few glazed eyeballs lifting up through picky black bangs. It looked and smelled like the Black Mass room in a cheap carnival haunted house. Anise and cut-rate incense stunk up the walls with little cauldrons of burning spices budding on the altar near the door.

"Hey guys," I said. "This is Sudsy."

"Hey," they chanted, low.

"How's it goin'?" said Miguel, our house's lead Goth.

Miguel and his girlfriend, Liz, shared the hundred-square-foot master bedroom which became their sacred space for sewing projects, dark music, and white magic. Wall-to-wall purple carpeting spread itself to the rounded corners. Flat surfaces held daggers and silver cups, crusty bowls of ramen, and locks of hair, piling up. I'd hear them sometimes on a weeknight while I watched teevee, when they'd wrap themselves in capes and close the door. I'd look out to see some special moon and know that worship was about to commence.

From under the crack it would pour, the sound of their shaking bodies spouting some gibberish like Wilton Bilder, only they were naked and using knives. The summoning of spirits seemed quite the process, always requiring a participant to re-cape and emerge, asking me for a pinch of sea salt or a pebble from the driveway. It was always about getting an item for protection inside of the circle, a part of their mass that I never understood. They had all the knives, what good was a pebble going to do? And why bother with calling forth evil if you needed to call forth protection first? As usual, I didn't recognize my creeping hypocrisy but I was about to learn fast — as I prepared to worship at the Altar of Sudsy, engaging in the blackest of magic — that protection never hurts, especially against the forces you summon yourself.

"How's it goin'?" repeated Miguel, looking Sudsy up and down from the back of an Absinthe haze. Sudsy's shaved head and black boots looked threatening, his Irish Catholic face beaming trouble all the time. He was in a mechanic's outfit and didn't dress like a skinhead, but was not far off from the gross queerboy SHARP (Skinheads Against Racial Prejudice) fetish that I still don't understand today. It's like wearing a pointed hood and expecting people to simply see it as a costume you find functional, your comfy white robe, with no allusion to being a racist. Miguel shuddered at the possible implications of Sudsy's high-laced stompers.

"You got any weed?" said Sudsy. That should have been a warning sign right there, bigger than all the Doc Marten's in the world, alerting me to drop to my knees and beg Gaia for protection.

"Huh?" Miguel was always shocked by impoliteness. Impoliteness and reggae.

"You got any weed? Ya know? Weed? Smoke? Ganja..."

"Yeah, Miguel, kick down," I said, interrupting before Sudsy had the chance to say "wacky tobaccy," ruining everything.

"Sorry, man," said Miguel. "I only got a little left." He held up his seeds and stems in a sad corner bag.

"So let's fuckin smoke it," said Sudsy.

"Yeah, let's all sit and smoke it!" I said, trying to ease the pain of my bringing an aggressive into the Goth house.

"I'm gonna save it," Miguel said. "For tomorrow." Even the people dramatically positioned on the fainting couches knew it was a lie, that there's no such thing as saving drugs for tomorrow.

"That's cool!" I lied. "Come on. Let's go, Sudsy." I just wanted to get him away from the party and into my room. He was volatile and drunk, and my misery was falling fast.

Sudsy mumbled under his breath as we walked away from the couch and cut a path for my room, which sat no bigger than a woodshed at the back of the circular house. There's a reason they don't sell many California Kings outside of California; in New England you'd have to split it into twelve pieces just to get it in the door. Futon Hut did a mean business.

There were some kids Goth dancing, pulling taffy near the stereo. I smiled and Sudsy tightened as we passed through them. I could see his bubble cracking, little veins whizzing across its surface. I didn't know Sudsy hated Goths or I would have come up the back stairs or just done it in the car, anything to avoid what was coming. But there were drugs in my room, drugs that I would not be saving for tomorrow or even later this morning, and I had to get to them.

In the kitchen was a smallish Goth with dreadlocks, little pencil ones with skulls twined in. He was muttering about injustice, his face down on the Formica table, left cheek sticky in white pancake and drool. An empty Chartreuse bottle rolled around at his feet, little canvas sneakers kicking its substantial glass. He was cute, the new Goth in my kitchen, with his sad-happy drunk talk. If I had come home alone, changing history, I may have made him coffee and patted his head. Instead I was with Sudsy, his face getting red, marching into my room.

"That fucker has weed… I seen that fucker before, at the bar," he said.

"Miguel? Yeah, he goes out sometimes. Sorry about that, I mean, maybe we can scrape my pipe."

"Fuck that, I wanna steal his weed. Fucker. With his stupid asshole hair and shitty funeral music, fuckin' losers…" Sudsy was a monster in grey coveralls. If he wasn't so cute I'd have thrown him out but I needed him. I needed an asshole and I needed the chaos and Sudsy more than fit the bill. With no protection, I had summoned the Devil himself.

Sudsy slipped into my life just like heroin had. I went looking for trouble and I got it, fell in love with it and allowed it to eat my heart. With heroin, it was that simple and that easy. It's the exact type of chaos I enjoy and crave. Therapists would later ask why I was there at rehab. I'd sit across from them like a husk, explaining that I was addicted to heroin. That's why I was there. It was right there in my chart: *opiate addicted*.

"But why are you self-medicating in the first place?" they'd all say.

"Because I love the medicine," was my stock reply. "I *enjoy* heroin."

Sudsy did his first heroin that night in my room with me, but I don't feel responsible for his later addiction. He was all part of it.

"What the hell is that stuff? Is that coke?" He lit up when I pulled one waxy bag out of its rubber-banded place in the bundle. The stamp on the bags showed Mickey Mouse with crossed out eyes and the word OVERDOSE underneath. Like Miguel and his pot, I wasn't really up for sharing but already I couldn't refuse Sudsy anything.

"Heroin," I said.

He tried to grab the bag out of my hand, a little kid grabbing for a bag of candy, but I pulled away, clutching the dope.

"Gimme!"

"Have you ever even…"

"Gimme it!"

"Sudsy, look. I'm going to do some then you can try a little of what's left, okay?" I knew I had the upper hand, even if only for small moments that never connected, they were so singular. When the stamped bag was in my hand, which it always was, things went my way.

"Okay. Make sure you save me some though."

"I will." I dumped the bag out onto a surface, and then used a matchbook cover to lift amounts of powder into a spoon. Sudsy went wild as I pulled out a needle, me putting on a puppet show of my life, showing off my amazing addict skills. I did mine in a shot and made him snort his, like I used to do. He wasn't ready and never would be.

After my shot I forgot about Sudsy until I heard some clunking around in my room. Opening up on my bed, I could see him standing over me, holding a clump of severed dreadlocks in his fist. Little pencil ones with skulls twined in. All the air sucked down into the floor.

"I cut it off!" he said, moshing around the tiny circle of my room, jubilant. "I cut his fuckin' ego off!" He hid the sad pile of knotted hair in my closet, on the shelf. "Lit-tle fuck-er!" Hahahaha!" Sudsy was punching me from the denial of my nod. "How's your hair, asshole! Hahaha! It's RIGHT THERE! Hahahaha!"

Words were gone. All I could picture was new Goth in the kitchen discovering his new haircut. Showing Miguel the stumps of his lost accomplishment. It was all over. What a loser Sudsy was with his shaved head, looking like a Marine and sneaking around the Goth house chopping off people's hair like a dictator, and now I'd have to move. I was sure of it.

I kept my eyes closed to avoid the ego-pile sitting in my closet. I hardly felt high anymore, there were so many new problems to deal with. Problems that hadn't existed before that night, before Sudsy. Replaying it in my mind I tried to reset it, to go back three hours. I would have never seen Sudsy, never danced with him at the weirdo bar, never taken him home or shared my dope. In the replay I take new Goth into my room and count his little dreadlocks like rosary prayers, waking up in the morning, getting high, and driving to TopQual like nothing ever happened.

Every time I opened my eyes they were still there on the shelf, flopping around like chopped worms. Sudsy had taped a few to his head and was now dancing the taffy pull and giggling to himself. It was still real. Sudsy had attacked someone inside my house, his hatred for sweetness and hair beading pushing up through his drunken skin until everybody felt the wrath. I needed more dope and fixed another.

Miguel's girlfriend began screaming from the kitchen and I was hoping for once that it was a giant rat but I knew. Sudsy opened my door to Miguel standing there, holding up new Goth and examining the damage. This is what Sudsy was waiting for. This is why he did it. He was mad about the pot. Miguel was his true target and the kid with the new haircut was collateral damage.

Sudsy's bubble turned solid murk; you could hardly see him inside as he grabbed the hair off the shelf and stuffed it into his hand, piece by piece, an evil clown magician. Maybe he's gonna put it back. Maybe it's a trick with a big *ta-daaah*. I was still on the bed, unbendable. If it was a trick it wasn't very good. As soon as Miguel opened his mouth Sudsy took two steps forward, quick, leaving his eyes rolling back in his head. I'd never been around much fighting and I could see the room fill with red.

Swinging his hair-packed fist, Sudsy laid a straight-on suckerpunch to Miguel's nose, knocking him to his back. Then Sudsy jumped on him like a rogue cop, punching through Miguel's hands, useless paws held shaking in front of his face.

"Where's… yer… weed… now… motha…fuckaaahh…" Sudsy swung with every word, Miguel's girlfriend screaming to the police dispatcher, "Hurry up! He's beating the shit… oh my god… hurry up! I don't know *who* he is… oh my god!"

I tried to turn invisible. I hardly knew Sudsy and I couldn't unpunch Miguel's poor face. Violence makes me shrink into a ball, a spineless vermin who is no help to anyone in the situation of attack. I couldn't jump out the window and I couldn't push through the wall of blood and mesh and I wanted to close the door.

Blue and red lights blared through from the street as the cruiser pulled up, people running in all directions to escape. Sudsy walked right down the front stairs to the cops, Miguel's blood dripping from the hair he still had in his hands.

"What's goin on, here?" asked the first pig, stopping Sudsy with a nightstick.

"Nothin' anymore… nothing's goin' on… I kicked his ass!" Sudsy laughed, pointing to Miguel bleeding out on the stoop, surrounded by a circle of angry Goths.

"He's a Nazi!" yelled new Goth's girlfriend. "He cut off all of Brian's hair! Look!"

Sudsy opened his hand. "Oh, yeah…" he said, "I cut that little Masshole's hair off… his ego, man… I cut his stupid ego clean off."

"Where you from?" asked the second, larger pig.

"Smith Hill, dude. I'm from right there on Smith Hill," Sudsy was pointing over an arch to a different neighborhood. "I grew up my whole life there. These little dicks are from Massachusetts. They ain't local, they're little Massholes, from way over there, Attleboro or some dumb shit…" He made the signal of a touchdown, like Massachusetts was on another planet.

I sat on the curb, between my housemates and the cop car. I could see new Goth, or Brian, as she called him, rubbing his head with his hand in shock. Not light shock but somebody-get-this-kid-a-space-blanket shock. He couldn't stop rubbing his head. I wanted to get him some Jet Black from inside to make it as better as I could, the kid just standing there, egoless. Maybe he would end up at Glitz Iz Hair! getting pushed on by Pleatherman's pointy fingers. God, I hope the cops don't search the house.

The pigs were as smitten with Sudsy as I was, proving once again that the police possess all the smarts of a misdirected teenage loser and the worst judgment in the world. Sudsy's spell was powerful on people who were in love, on drugs, drunk with power, or any combination of the three, and the pigs, just like me, played right into his hands.

The big one pulled him to the side. "Okay. Look, pal, I'm gonna put ya in the car but ya ain't getting booked. I'm gonna drive to the station and after you hop out, you take your ass straight back to the Hill."

"Yes, sir," shouted Sudsy, climbing into the open door like he'd done this more than a few times. He laughed while he sat in the back of the car, craning his neck to see the Goth house, feeling vindicated in his assumed arrest. He heard their yelling and went berserk, bugging his eyes out and licking his middle fingers. Making the blow-job sign.

"Fascist!" they screamed. "Fuckin' animal!"

My upstairs neighbor got involved from her window. She knew the cops and she couldn't stand Miguel or his girlfriend. "I didn't see it but I sure did hear it… and I tell ya, Bobby, I bet that little shit deserved it… let that one go, huh? The one with my friend on the curve there?" She pointed at me. "Nice kid. He helps out." I had no idea what she was talking about. I helped her with her groceries once, maybe that. "I'm tellin' ya," she hocked up a loogie and shot it on to the steps next to Miguel. "I'm tellin ya… that one musta asked for it."

But he hadn't. Miguel hadn't done much of anything except withheld pot from a guest. That's not out of the ordinary. New Goth Brian did nothing at all, just sat there looking sad and adorable with all his hair attached. Something was wrong with Sudsy, some disconnect on a scope I'd never seen. So much rage, I wish he'd have taken it out on a proper target like a beanbag chair or the Pope rather than the small quiet Goths of Providence, who I'd never be able to live with again. One night and Sudsy was already blowing everything up, and I walked into his glamorous explosion hoping to be a tourist for a while.

My mother said yes when I asked if I could move back in for a while.

"Yuht," she said, "but you better keep a job, Francis!" She was making her meatballs, her hands crunching ground pork together with ground beef, eggs whites sliding gelatinous down her forearms. "What happened at QualTop, anyways?"

"TopQual said they didn't need me anymore," I said. I couldn't tell the truth, that I had quit TQ the day after the first blast of Sudsy, I couldn't imagine going back now that I had a new commotion to concentrate on. I'd get a café job, and with all the money I saved on rent, I'd be able to do heroin at will, I thought. It wouldn't be so bad to live back at home, and since I was just making eighteen I figured it didn't make me a loser like anyone else who moved back in with their parents.

"No teevee shows?"

"No, Ma. That's over." It was, too. No more shows, no more TopQual, no more sublet. Back to square one, at least until I could figure something out.

At my parents' house everything was still in place, the red shades, my waterbed, even my poster wall had been left intact as if my mother knew I'd be back. But she was also the person who left the Christmas lights stuffed into the bushes year-round so maybe it was something more like that. Either way, I had a room to stay in and a car to get me to Providence. Now I'd shoot for that art career.

I stole a few pencil boxes from Mira's room before the Goths chased me out with a baseball bat, and I would draw on lined paper, trying to create a portfolio to get me into an art school full time. Just like Clown College, it would never work out as I'd planned.

Sudsy would stay over with me at my parents' house on weekends, my mother on one occasion absentmindedly bringing towels in to what had been an empty room, walking straight into the Filth of Gay Sex. No light oral passive to witness, it was full on when the door opened, the waves of the waterbed undulating with sodomy.

"Oops!" she said, backing away rather than turning around.

"Fuck!" said Sudsy.

"Don't worry about it," I said. "She's fine."

And she was. Her capacity for blocking things out as they happened had been honed over the years to an instantaneous reaction. Witness, block, forget, gone. This was how she had stayed with my dad and his alcohol for this long. When he finally did get sober after a one-time visit to a 30-day detox, she had nothing in her memory bank to hold against him. He was new. As was I, a new person in my old room, and in her mind I was not engaging in The Sodomy, but instead thanking her for the clean towel delivery. All she saw was her little clown and his sleep-over pal, and through the powerful filter of her recall, we were still just making toast.

"Youse guys gonna get up?" she said through the particle board door.

"Yup!" said Sudsy, already dressed in last night's beer-soaked coveralls.

"Yup!" I said, rolling over the lip of my waterbed, laughing at Sudsy.

"She's fine," I told him. "I'm tellin ya. You want some breakfast?"

Sudsy would linger almost as long as heroin would. We stayed together for three years, on and off. Mostly off. He couldn't be depended upon for anything other than snorting my wake-up or stealing my sisters gold chain. Sudsy was good at the pawn shop, always charming two more dollars out of the guy. Between the two of us, both living at home with our respective families, we became the most hated couple in Providence. The Goths had taken to traveling with a bat wherever they went, and spent a lot of time defacing promo posters for Sudsy's band, Skank Brigade, by writing FASCISTS! or NAZIS! over the picture of his kick drum.

The city of Providence was still my home despite the economic need to sleep in my childhood bed and I would drive there every day to work at a café on Wickenden Street, where I served fancy coffee and gelato to the children of Diane von Furstenberg or Diana Ross. I would hide whenever someone with black clothes walked in until the Goth situation blew over. I wanted to apologize to the kid with the haircut and help him with new style decisions but he had moved to Boston with Miguel's girlfriend and cat. He stole them both.

Soon the whole Goth House would follow suit, most everyone who had been there for the bloodbath moving to Boston to hang out in new clubs, gaining apartments and a new access to genuine fetish gear. I would stay in my bedroom at my mom's, plotting how to keep myself stocked up on heroin, how to keep Sudsy at bay, and how to turn my new found café job into a viable art career, or any career at all.

I didn't have money for college. I figured I'd do some part-time night classes so I could at least feel a little collegiate. I took out student loans and began attending the Rhode Island School of Design. That's right, RISD, which cost a million dollars for two credits. I learned the fine art of crayon and glue screen printmaking which I already knew how to do from ninth grade public school art class so I really shined.

I wasn't an official student, I mean, I didn't go to RISD during the daytime or anything. I was in Continuing Education. I was a local, a kid from Woonsocket paying an exorbitant amount to take night classes for an arbitrary certificate. I don't know. It was never really explained to me. All I wanted was that big folding carrying case they had in the RISD store, a giant, flat black pleather case, in which I would be carrying sketches. There were kids carrying all kinds of sketches, sketch-carriers, pen sets, and silk charmeuse. Making things. Doing stuff. I pictured myself carrying all kinds of stuff. A busy, busy artist.

During the daytime session when the real artist kids were running up and down steps with brushes and easels, the continuing education crowd would gather on the campus to soak it in, sitting in the cafeteria surrounded by old money and kids who were so white they were transparent, blue blood running through thin veins, all visible through a shell of the finest alabaster flesh.

Guys like Alexandre, who happened to be going through a "creative phase" and his parents needed somewhere to stick his ass between prep school and grad school. You know the type — Alexandre is focusing on performance art so for the next four years you'll be seeing him around campus doing wacky things with grapes and mayonnaise.

Wow, Alex, I didn't know you were in the performance department! I wicked love the performance department because I wicked love performance art! I love the performance you do every day around this time, it must be a series or something. You know the one, the one where you walk into the campus coffee shop and sit at that big table with all your friends and act like an asshole? I wicked love that one. It's so powerful. Throw in a few Tampax and an old ice cream scooper and you have one hell of a performance there, Al...

Continuing education sucked. If I saw one more "performance" out of Alex I would commit homicide. Now aimless and lacking in career opportunities, I did what any sensible faggot would do. I enrolled in The Marco Botelo School of Cosmetology and Hair Design. It's very exclusive. All the best hairdressers went there. I threw myself into it wholeheartedly and took it dead serious: Beauty College.

I had to wear white on white, with a white smock thrown over the whole number to add an air of professionalism. I looked nothing like Mira. One of the Golden Rules at my beauty school was learning to use the word "mousse" as a noun, an adjective, and — most importantly — a verb: *Mousse it, Debbie.*

The campus was on Federal Hill, a very exclusive Italian neighborhood in Providence. You may have heard of it from movies. Very fancy. And all the students were top notch and boy, have they gone far. Look at Darrin Barrichione, for Christ's sake, he's an assistant manager at the salon inside Wal-Mart. And not the one on North Main St, either. The big one Downcity. Friggin' superstar.

All of the instructors at the school were to be addressed as Miss this or Miss that, like Miss Kathy and Miss Laura Lee. More like Miss Guided or Missed the Bus. Not to mention Missed the Match on that foundation. These biddies were supposed to teach us about fashion but here they stood in these hideous outfits: stretchy Lycra pants with stirrups tucked into a pair of pastel flats, the bottom half topped off with a sweatshirt with the screen-printed image of puppies in a basket or a Christmas tree with a battery-powered star that would blink for the holidays. Festive yet sensible because what is a beauty professional without seasonal accessories? Not a team player, that's for sure.

Every day began with Cosmetology Theory which was rote recitation, each student reading a paragraph or two out of *Milady's Standard*, which is the Bible of Beauty. Theory time would draw groans from the classroom as the students would stumble over words like "parasitic" and "elasticity." God forbid Gina would get a sentence with the word "esthetician" in it, the pain could last a full minute. Fortunately we weren't there to quibble over grammar and would move on to hands-on practical training, called *practical*.

Pin curls, finger waves, and mock color applications were performed over and over on the mannequin heads that were issued to us on the first day. The mannequin heads said "manikin" on the bottom, and each had a little metal nameplate fastened to the neck with rivets. All of the mannequin heads came with the name "Val" which I thought was a little too vague so I changed my mannequin head's name to "Monette," kind of a sassy French thing that would better match her make-up.

Upon graduation, Monette's face was burned off with a welding torch and her flaming head thrown off the top of Sh'Booms. You may not have heard of it but Sh'Booms was the hottest club among the Providence baby-boomers. Press your poodle skirt, grab a Zima, and get dancing! Don't be scared, do that electric slide as if your life depended on it. A lot of the kids from Marco Botelo's would meet at Sh'Booms after a long day of color theory, which was always taxing.

Color day gave the students an opportunity to really sparkle. The school would be abuzz as the last bits of Miss Clairol were rinsed and flushed down the sink. People would run from classroom to classroom showing off their new dye jobs. *Oh my God, Gina dyed her hair that new color, dark dark dark, it looks wicked good.*

Oh my God did you friggin' see Karen Porcelli? She dyed her hair that new color, you know that new red, it's kinda like eggplant or something, you know, that new red? It's wicked nice, why, no? They would get so excited that they'd stumbled upon a color that hadn't existed, not in nature, not on the color wheel; it was a brand new color.

Karin Porcelli drove one of those Geo Trackers or a Jeep or another brand of easy to flip cheerleader decapitators. It was another one of those new colors. *That new green.*

Do you like my Jeep, Geener?

On my first day at Marco Botelo, I stumbled late into the classroom and found myself a seat. It was right in the middle of the room, dead center with the instructor. Names and fun facts were being exchanged. I assumed it was the standard Let's Go Around The Room And Introduce Ourselves format: "Hi, my name is ____ and I like ____."

"My name's Tanya and… I don't know! I'm seventeen? Is that something about me?"

"Yes, Tanya! That is something!" The instructor had her name written on the board behind her. I copied it down in my new notebook: *Miss Laura-Lee.*

Miss Laura-Lee seemed a little out of place at Marco Botelo but her father owned the building, showing how far down nepotism actually reaches. The students were going wild. She couldn't control her classroom. It was the first hour of the first day and already people were giving her shit. Sleeping on their desks, snapping their gum, the class establishing its Alpha's right away. They separated into cliques, all definable. The Go Getters, the Quiet Ones, the Nice Girls, the Mean Girls.

The other boy in the class, in an attempt to ingratiate himself with the Mean Girls, renamed Miss Laura-Lee as Miss Lindy-Lou — a name that stuck for some reason despite its lack of bite. Miss Laura-Lee / Miss Lindy-Lou. Not funny but, again, it stuck.

The way the class was going, I had a hard time garnering respect for Miss Laura-Lee. The people in the next classroom were laughing and carrying on. I should be in that class, I thought, with no intention of trying to establish myself as the class clown in this cluster of hairspray. They wouldn't get it.

This became clear on the sixth day of classes, the first Monday of the second week. Some girl named Sůe was talking to her friend, Missy, in the hallway. They were both Nice Girls, the kind of girls my sister used to call *sweet peas* in high school. Sue was a sweet pea. Coming in from the smoking area, I heard the end of their conversation:

"Nuh-uh."

"Yuh-huh, Missy! I saw him get dropped off by a guy this morning, his booooyfriend!"

"Naah-uh," Missy sucked at her teeth. "It coulda been his brother, Sue. Jeez…" She whipped out her paddle brush and two-foot can of shaper spray and began upward maneuvers.

"Do *you* make out with your brother? 'Cause I don't." Sue cracked herself up. Then they both laughed. "Isn't it *weird*? Isn't it *weird* that Frank is gay?" Sue said, really loud.

I passed into them, into the echo of their laughs, the final bursts of sticky aerosol landing on my nose.

"That was Sudsy. He's my boyfriend. We totally do it."

Sue froze; Missy ran away. I moved myself into the classroom and took my seat, nestled between the other boy and Missy, who wouldn't look at me anymore. Not that we were pals before this but now she was going out of her way to avoid my stare, unrelenting.

"Open your books to page 17." Miss Laura Lee slid her flats off under the desk.

Sue must've told all the students about her grand faux pas before class began because it seemed like everyone was looking at me, waiting for something, like I was going to blow my top, deep faggot style, snapping in circles and stuff. I'm sure they'd seen the movies but "two snaps up" was all new to them at the time. Probably even newer to me.

This was pre-cell phone, pre-computer. Everything still had to be looked up manually: to find out if it was raining outside you took yourself outside to check. If you didn't know the lyrics to a song you made them up — my sister thought in Prince's "Little Red Corvette" that he sang *Pay The Rent, Colette* which made no sense at all but she really thought those were the correct lines. MTV had Boy George and Pete Burns but nobody questioned their sexuality. The American Hypnosis Machine makes it so these people aren't queer, but *queer* as in *a little off*.

"Well, I'll be goddamned. That Indian from the Village People, he was a gay! They were all gays!" People really said that in the '70s. Like Paul Lynde and Charles Nelson Reilly before them, these people demanded a state of denial from the entire US, paving the way for new queers like Sam Harris on *Star Search*. It took everything I had not to scream out in class everything that had happened in the hall. I was holding it in like a tic.

To not be the Village People, I needed to find protection at Marco Botelo. I didn't want to be a novelty and I sure as hell didn't want to be tolerated. I needed to find a hag. Just as science was hell-bent on proving homosexuality to be genetic, and sexuality and gender to be mercurial, so was I in suggesting that the Fag Hag was Born That Way, too. The existence of the fag hag is nature not nurture, and serves as a built-in, universal support system for a lost fagboy.

I'm glad that hags can be out of the closet these days and don't have to go on pretending, being dragged into loveless relationships as someone's beard. *No more beards!* is what my sign at the Fag Hag Visibility Rally reads. *This is bullshit!*

Sue would definitely not be my hag. Missy either, though I had initial hopes that she may be a comrade. While Miss Laura Lee was talking about page 17, I was filling the borders of page 18 with doodles of different classmates. It was harmless until my pen got to Sue.

I drew a vicious portrait of her, beyond caricature; the hair went up into the margins of the top of the page and her face was drawn coming in at a sharp angle from both ears with a razor-blade nose, a hatchet face. I drew her full face and even I would admit it came out well. Some of my better work, it looked just like her. I should have left the caricature alone but I missed that the whole point of caricature, I guess, is that it's up to the viewer to decipher whose attached earlobes they're looking at, not filling in too many blanks for them. I had to go further, drawing her nametag on her cartoon smock: SUE in bubble letters, just like her real name tag. Placed in a thought bubble over her head, and creeping into the paragraph on scabies, I wrote "Isn't that wicked weird about Frank being GAY?" removing all doubt should someone wonder about the identity of the drawing's subject.

"Okay, that's lunch, then!" Miss Laura Lee said. "Be back in a half an hour. Not an hour. Not thirty-five minutes. How long?"

"A half-hour," repeated two students at the front.

I tucked my textbook into my bag with all of my stuff and went out to my car to smoke a joint. Sudsy was out there at my car, inexplicably waving six bags of dope fanned out. I didn't ask how but I made him give me three so I could get beyond the normal territory of stasis, maybe get a little loaded. It was only the first week, it's not like we'd be handling scissors or coloring someone's hair after lunch. I slid back in at the thirty-five minute mark. Miss Laura Lee said nothing as I took my place next to Missy. *Little Missy*.

"Frank, can I talk to you?" Miss Laura Lee said. She had lettuce from lunch in her hair.

"Francis," I said.

"Okeeey, Francis, is it? You think we could talk outside the classroom for a minute? Bring your textbook."

I almost collapsed. Little shit Missy was grinning as I took the book out of my bag and went out into the hallway. I could hear Sue crying and knew I was in for it.

"Frank…"

"Francis. Fran-siss. No *Frank*."

Usually a teacher would say "*Someone* told me this…" or "*I* overheard…" placing themselves squarely in the line of accepted blame rather than blow the anonymity of the fink. Miss Laura Lee wasn't that good. "Over lunch, Missy went into your bag and showed Sue something in your book that made her very upset…"

"She went in my BAG?"

"Oh, yeah, she… see, she… she said…"

"I don't care what she said, she went into my shit without my permission!" I was turning the tables while I had a chance.

"Yes, well…"

"Well what, Miss Laura Lee? Well, she shouldn't have done that?

Well, she should be reported as a thief? Well, she better not even look at me when we go back in there? Well what?" I was barking at her now. The more I defended my actions, the more horrified I was that I had been violated. Now I was passionate that Little Missy should be the one getting lectured, not me, and it only took a minute to convince Miss Laura Lee.

"Sue seems *very* upset," she said.

"Sue's a dipshit."

"Can I see it?"

"What?"

"Can I see the cartoon? Is it funny?"

"I thought so."

"Let me see it." Miss Laura-Lee was chomping at the bit to see what I'd done.

I opened up to page 18 and showed her my handiwork. The scribbly pen lines had been mucked up a little by Sue's stupid tears but the image and the sentiment were still well intact. Miss Laura Lee covered her mouth to avoid letting out a shriek of laughter.

"OhMyGodItLooksJustLikeHer!" she said, buckling at the knees. She was really hooting about it, bracing herself on the wall to catch her breath before heading back in, the lettuce dropping from her perm. "Whoooo. Okeeey. Whoooo. Ah, okeeey, let's go back in," she grabbed my hand in hers and led me towards the door. Sue and Missy were smiling when we walked in, they were so sure I had gotten ass-reamed.

I moved my seat five feet behind Missy and to the left, to get away from her and so I could keep an eye on her. They were both waiting for my public apology for my cartoon but instead Miss Laura Lee brought my textbook back to me and placed it on my desk.

"Nobody is to go into *anyone's* things, EVER, not over lunch, not after hours, not *ever*," she said. Most of the class seemed confused but I couldn't hide my happiness. Sue and Missy exchanged nervous glances as I opened back up to page 19 and began a new cartoon, this time of Little Missy.

By the time I was nearing graduation from Marco Botelo, the administration had no place to put me, I had missed so many days. They called that "extending." I was an extender. By then, I was an extending extender. I was there longer than some of the staff, who I now considered my peer group. I couldn't tie myself, smock or no smock, to the other students.

I had finally found my hag, Deleena, but she got expelled for punching the Dean of students. Deleena was actually an old hag of mine, we grew up together. Deleena had been beating people up since third grade. "One more word, Miss Violet, and I'll *drop* you," she said. I knew she wasn't lying.

As the reaction began to pass Miss Violet's lips, Deleena's giant hand came out of nowhere. She had beautiful hands, real piano fingers laying on one of those slaps that sounds like a punch but leaves fingerprints so you know it was a slap. Miss Violet hit the floor. She got *dropped*. It's not like she didn't get warned but I can't see anyone get hit, as my only two possible reactions are nervous laughter or quick retreat. I did both, snorting out of the room as Miss Violet fished with a ruler under the file cabinets where her headband had slid as an aftershock of the slap.

Even though The Dean loathed me, I felt horrible for her. That was really mean, I thought in the bathroom where I found empathy. Seeing her on all fours trying to find that damn headband, she wasn't The Dean anymore but the victim of a bitch slap, this little person brushing hair off her dusty tweed jacket and trying to reassemble her headband. It had colorful thread and pewter bells on it. Her grandson had made it for her. Yay for gay kids! I tried to help Miss Violet find the last bell but it was gone. Deleena never came back.

After her expulsion I was friendless. There was nobody else to laugh with. Everyone was new. A roll of new students began every six weeks. I'd see them through orientation and attend their graduation ceremonies every six weeks. I tried to make friends with the new boy in the freshmen class, a boy who was also named Francis. Stupid Saints, I mean Jesus Christ, can't one French-Canadian parent name their kid Astro or Pluto or anything non-biblical? (No.) Everyone had saint names in my school. I did know a boy named Brad in junior high. He was younger than me and super cute. I was going to tell him but he died before I got the chance. Some horrid kid cancer.

"Hi, I'm Francis," I said. "You new here?"

"Oh. Hi. I'm Francis," he said, with no recognition of our same name, ignoring the bonding opportunity. He didn't say. "I'm Francis, too," or "No way!" I tried to come up with a small riff off it, something clever, but I couldn't think of anything so I just said "Hi" again. "Hi Francis," I said. That's all.

Other Francis began the assessment of me, scanning from shoes to hair, bottom to top. Without once looking in my eyes he had decided I didn't pass muster. I wasn't his level of gay, what with my skippy sneakers and drug habit. He was gleaming white in his new school uniform; you could tell he would just screech when it got dirty.

Not only was my uniform soiled and ripped, cigarette smoke had turned it to an off- white, and my smock smelled like an ashtray, with burnholes all up and down. My skin smelled like bleach and heroin and Vitamin B, and it became apparent in my last days as a Beauty School Student that the only eyes that would look into mine would be the painted rubber eyes of my mannequin head, Monette.

When I wasn't hiding in one of the many bathrooms, I'd stick around the clinic area working on Monette. Those heads are supposed to last six months at best but Monette was different, a direct reflection of myself. She thought she was a warrior and she wasn't going down. Even after two years, she still hadn't hit her dead-eyed bottom. Her head leaned ten degrees off-kilter, sitting too loose on the metal pole that was inserted into the hole in her base. She lolled about on the base that was screwed to the table next to all the other mannequin heads — the Vals with their perfect neck posture. Monette was a hag. My hag. All gravelly-voiced and whiskey-smelling, Monette got around. All the Vals knew about Monette, and although not one of them aspired to be her, they all knew who she was and that was good enough for the both of us.

She looked good. While most other students left the faces of their Val heads intact, I removed Monette's make-up with paint thinner and re-applied a new Goth look, with magic marker mascara painted in clumps under her eyes. Black lips. Her hair was cotton candy from all the bleach jobs and re-dyes I'd given her over the years. I liked the way her remaining strands were yellow at the roots and olive green at the ends, fading into shiny black.

"Oh my god, Gina, did you see what that Frank guy did to his Val doll?" the other Francis said.

"Right? I know! He's freakin' retahded… I've known him since I started last year and he's a freakin' weeeiahd-o. You'll see, he's weird, like *gross* weird, *and* he calls his Val head '*Monette*'! Whadda faggot, with his stupid French doll head. Look at her ugly face!"

"I know!" said Other Francis.

That was it. I looked up at them to let them know I heard what they said. *Call me faggot all you want,* I told them, *but do not fuck with Monette. She can't defend herself.*

The clinic at Marco Botelo was the only part of the school that wasn't windowless. The bright white waiting area had wrap-around pleather couches and a smattering of old magazines — *Good Housekeeping, Better Homes & Gardens, Reader's Digest* — nothing about hair and nothing too racy. The occasional *Glamour* would slip in but it would always be stolen within an afternoon.

The appointment book was fueled by women and men who lived in one of the three old folks' homes on the block. Once a week they would come in for their wash and set, press and curl, or beard trim. It was something they could do, a small thing to keep some dignity among the bedpans and thieving nurses. To feel pretty, to be clean-shaven. To be touched. To hear cuss words and get mad, to get gossip and share stories. Every one of them had the most incredible stories but sometimes I wasn't able to believe them.

It's like riding Greyhound. Clients lie or inflate. I think a good bunch of them were embellishers but they earned it. The stories weren't coming out of nowhere; they were all rooted in truth. People were different then, even the old folks. Not like the sociopath clients of today who lie about the smallest things. Having an internet persona's bigger than a house, it's hard for today's client to slip with decorum into the real world. They've honed their shtick to the point where they don't know how to act when in a non-virtual situation, how to utilize the ego in reality.

Recently I watched a client helping his kid with her homework — something I'd always pictured being done at a kitchen island with granite countertops, both mentor and student sitting behind big, cozy mugs of hot chocolate — but instead they sit in my chairs and text the answers from their smartphones, answers they got from Wikipedia. I bet my pepere and father said this same stuff after the television was invented. *That goddam teevee is gonna rot your brain*, my father would say. Pepere would mutter in Canuck, pacing around with his hands behind his back, counting rosary beads. I never saw my pepere watch teevee.

The clients of Marco Botelo had no such distractions, no smart phones, no vid screens, leaving the brunt of their identity unfiltered, attentive, and present while you brushed thin hairs towards patches of skin. They would come in weekly for wash and sets and temporary rinses. The rinses used at the school were made by a company called Miss Roux, a division of Clairol. The colors in the swatch book ranged from deep brown to light brown, and then you'd flip the worn pages to reveal the blondes. Purple blonde, pink-blonde, and blue-blonde, the last one being the origin of the term "blue-hairs."

Blue-hairs — the community of those with bluish hair — don't just wake up that way. Blue hair doesn't spring from the scalp. They work for that shit. The blue color of their namesake, which ranges from a powder blue to a deep steel, comes from applying a blue rinse over white hair to cut the yellow. I don't know why nobody at Glitz Iz Hair knew that. Basic color theory: complementary colors dull each other out when mixed. So if your white hair looks like rusty water, I'll grab for the violet rinse to cut the orange.

The rinses were lined up according to name and number on the shelves inside the dispensary. Every day, one student would be assigned to operate the dispensary and another assigned to the front desk. I always wanted to be in the dispensary and would argue for the position. It had a door that closed and a service window like an ice cream shop. The students would have to come for me to get the colors, perms, bob pins, and rinses to use on their clients. Anything that was worth more than two dollars was kept guarded in the dispensary.

I spent hours organizing the colors. Miss Roux was my favorite, with animal-named shades like Frivolous Fawn, White Minx, and Pretty Beaver. Nothing made my day like someone telling me they needed some Pretty Beaver. The non-animal color names weren't as fun but some of them sounded dirty: Hidden Honey, Bashful Blonde, Chocolate Kiss, Black Rage. The color titles hinted at a suspected personality trait of the person who wore that shade: the girls who got Black Rage were dead serious, and it was never dark enough; Hidden Honeys were picky, it was either too gold or not gold enough; Bashful Blondes were low-maintenance, they didn't care to make waves. Too bashful.

When I was on the clinic floor I would always choose my clients. The other students would run from most work as I often would but I was the go-to volunteer for all the clients who nobody else would touch.

Jawa would come in every two weeks, less often than the nursing home ladies but with the same regularity, sending everyone but me running for the doors. If he wasn't seven feet tall, he wasn't two feet. His hair fell below the middle of his back in one big nest, a saggy ginger beehive with a halo of baby hairs encircling his face. He didn't talk much, only necessary words. On his visits he would cram his frame into my chair for the consultation, an obligatory part of the process. I always knew what he wanted.

The bouffant that Jawa got challenged anything I had ever seen, even on teevee. My mother had a huge blonde bouffant in the '60s, frosted and swirled and lacquered. When I see the pictures I want to scream, so grateful to have been nurtured by that wig. With Jawa I didn't feel such honor. Jawa was mean and the students were smart to run.

He was legendary for being the guy who took a shit in the shampoo chair during an especially relaxing crème rinse. His medications must have been laid on heavy that day; the teacher who was there says he was "real out of it." Jawa's shit episode made an amazing story, true or not, the wonderful mix of scatology and cosmetology keeping students talking for years.

They probably still talk about Jawa and the brown puddle of stink that followed him that day. As the story went, Miss Dot chased him out of the school with two rolls of Bounty in her hands, screaming how she wasn't gonna clean it up. Jawa was 86ed for a full year until the students who bore witness graduated out.

With all the shit talk surrounding Jawa, I understood why the others didn't want to touch him but for me there was no sense in resistance. I saw in Jawa the same sadness I saw in myself though his was deeper, some deep ancient Capricorn sadness that can't be figured out it's so old. It's just there, hanging like stars. Jawa didn't stay quiet because he had nothing to say. I'd imagine he was full of interesting information. He stayed quiet because he knew if he said something out loud it would become real and make him die a little more.

Not like secrets or anything, but more of daily life. Jawa could never tell you a story about watching someone eat alone or seeing a baby bird hatch without welling up and trying to hold back, the fine needles of tears pressing against the inside of his eyelids, peripheral lightning bolts bleeding out to rims of fire.

It's awful to go through life that way, when you know you have this cloud. Where most other people can look at a bunny and simply think, Oh, look, a bunny, Jawa would see the entire life cycle of the bunny spelled out in a millisecond. He would consider the rabbit's mother, wonder if she was still alive or if she had been mangled by a RIPTA bus, the giant Volvo tires crushing her back legs while her baby ran into the bushes.

Jawa would wonder if the bunny had enough to eat or if it belonged to someone, who would take care of it now that its mother was dragging herself to the gutter with her front legs? Jawa saw the death in everything and it tore him apart string by string. Rabbits, old people, children: they all took a pull at the threads of his psychic hem, steady unraveling.

I was glad he didn't say much once he got into my chair. Not even a Hello. He'd just look at me and nod, and I'd get to work on the combing of his hair pile, separating it into manageable chunks and then slowly pulling the knots out of each sub-section. He wasn't tender-headed. Physically he was an ox. Emotionally he was like me, probably head-frozen at an early age.

Jawa's history was gleaned not from words but from vibration, the insight harvested when shampooing a head, my hands pressed flat against the scalp. This is how it is with all clients but with Jawa it was like a flood as soon as I'd touch him so I'd pull my shield into a tight mesh. There was some recognizable veil he chose to place over his emotions daily in order to avoid the pain of bunnies; I wasn't sure what it was and would never ask but I was glad it was there.

I couldn't imagine how strong the pull of his sadness would be had it not been dulled by the screen of medication. We both lived inside of screen porches, only we used different materials to build them. Jawa's screen was thicker than mine so I figured him to require a chemical with a long half-life. Probably methadone.

I could imagine he was like me in the morning, waking up with a yelp, his still sleeping fists swinging at the phantoms that lurk outside of eyelids, hoping for a small crack. Before his massive feet hit the floor he's already thinking of the dirty dishes piling up in the other room, the people he owes, the people that owe him, and the amount of refills he has remaining on his prescriptions.

He keeps his head on the pillow as the wretched swirl of thoughts begins again: poverty, beauty, violence, animals, long lines, missed appointments, case workers, single baby shoes in the gutter. They all dance in a kick line before him until the meds are absorbed and assimilated, until a gray Mylar gel is rubber-banded to the edge of the spotlight. Dulled, the high-kicks aren't as drastic, the music one long drone. It's the same light only muffled. Over fifteen minutes, terror subsides to panic, panic morphs into fear until fear turns to dullness, and within this dullness, new worries begin to seep.

I brought in my sister to be my hair model for the final test to get my Cosmetology license. The Big State Board test. Written and then Practical. Questions and then Operations.

On State Board day, all the other girls were put together tight. Clean smocks, clear eyes, and a fresh kit to use. Inside each of their kits were nice sharp scissors, Ziploc bags full of sanitized perm rods, color bottles, and manicuring implements. They all looked well rested and, unlike me, none of them were visibly bleeding.

The night before my test, out I went drinking to excess, not allowing myself to trip out on the reality of test-taking but instead pushing it all to the back burner with the barricade of alcohol. Real mill-town drinking, shots and beers, drinking and driving, an entire kitchen crew ending up at a waitress's house after the bars closed, a fridge full of lite beer being ripped into.

The hostess asked me to run outside to the garage to get a Tom Petty cassette from her car, said she wanted to hear that song *Freefalling*. She didn't tell me there was a six-foot garage pit there, a giant hole in the ground yawning between the entrance to the garage and the Tom Petty tape.

My vision left me as my ribs raked against the old cement of the pit, following my ripped-up shins. For a second I thought I went blind, landing squarely on my feet inside the dark hole, the alcohol and opiates masking the thump of bruised ribs and the electric screams from my shins. I wasn't blind. I could see light above me. Had I not been drunk, I would have died.

You know that story? Of how your bones are more rubbery when you're super-wasted? It's true. You could dive off a ladder head first and just carry on, bloody and fuzzed out until the next day when everyone says, *You're lucky you were wasted! You woulda died* and you wonder how the connection isn't made in their brains. Like how I wouldn't have gone anywhere to get anyone a Tom Petty tape, ever, unless I had been drunk in the first place. How I wouldn't have fell in the pit. How

I wouldn't even be in the same town as this pack of professional losers unless I was wasted. None of this was considered from the bottom of the pit. Nothing broken, I heaved myself up the rock wall and walked back in the house.

"Here's your tape. Thanks for telling me about the hole…" Blood was pouring from six different spots on my body, the cloth of my outfit clinging sticky to the red gashes. The room of alcoholics took a collective inhalation, all of their eyes growing out of their heads at the sight of me. Upon exhalation was a roaring boozy laughter coming from all sides.

"Oh my God," said the hostess, "no friggin WAY."

"I thought I was dead."

"You could have been dead. Are you okay?" She was terrified. My father was her insurance agent, home and auto, and garage pits were not allowed. Illegal. Realizing that she pushed me to fall into an illegal hole in her garage, she was worried I would sue. I could have. Had it been ten years later, with the acceptance of litigiousness rising and everyone suing everyone, I could be living in her house today, driving her stupid car. I could have everything she had and sell it for the money.

"I don't think I'm dead. I think I'm fine." I was laughing now, too. Something about the fall sobered me up, the pain shooting into my legs removing the syrup from my synapses. "I need to go home… what time is it? Shit… shit shit shit… I have my test tomorrow morning." All of a sudden it was all too much, the reality. The biggest test of my life was in four hours and the only preparation I had completed was not dying the night before.

"Can I give you a ride? Are you going to tell your father?"

"My father?"

"Yeah, my brother put that garage pit in to work on his Austin Healey and I told him, 'Make sure you cover that thing up!' But he never listens. You know him? My brother? He's an asshole."

"I'm not telling anyone, not gonna sue you or your ugly brother. And I'll walk home. You guys are too wasted." The blood had made me sober and self-righteous.

I needed stitches and money so I should have gone to the hospital and sued but my career was calling. I had to get home and assemble my kit for the test, something that should have been done six months ago and now had to be crammed into a three-hour window. I always do this. The other students would have the perfect kits.

You can rent pre-assembled kits from a company called Rent-A-Kit. The pristine kits the others were sure to have would be rentals. The smart way to go. My kit was thrown together with remnants from beauty school and anything I could find in my mother's cabinets. On the way to take the test I stopped at a CVS to buy everything else I would need. CVS doesn't have most of that stuff.

When we got into the room, the test lady gave the instructions and screwed the dial on an egg-timer. We had ten minutes to set up our stuff in silence. All the girls had the same kits, the dream kits containing perfect little rectangle towels, stacks of them, all bleachy and clean.

I had one beach towel, six feet by four feet. It had Pig Pen from the *Peanuts* comics on it. It said *Cleanliness Is Next To Impossible* in his thought bubble. My sister laughed when I took it out of the plastic bag and wrapped it around her head, stacking it like the turban of a high holy man.

"You're such a dork, Francis!"

"Shhhh! ...you have to be quiet or I fail."

"Yeah. Good luck with that." My sister was comparing my kit to the kits of the other students. She was right. I couldn't have been less prepared. In the testing room you're supposed to be quiet as a monk, all of your stuff laid out and sanitized. With each operation they threw at me on it got worse.

By the time I had to perform a mock color application using cholesterol in a tint bottle, I realized that I didn't have cheap scissors to snip the tip off the cap, allowing for the mock solution to flow out onto my sister's head. I looked around the room for a face I knew. On my left was Zenieda, a girl I had graduated with. She had everything laid out like a pro.

"Pssst..." I was waking my arms like a chimp. "Pssssssst! Hey! Pssssst... hey... Zenieda... hey Z, psssst, hey..."

"WHAT?" she mouthed.

"Do you have cheap scissors I can use to snip this?" I mimed the snipping motion.

"NO." Her model looked at my sister in her *Peanuts* head-wrap and rolled her eyes at us, whispering something to Zenieda. The only word I could make out was *loser*.

"Fuck you," I mouthed, as if this was any time to need to get the last word in. Of course she had cheap scissors. She was a cheap girl.

Zenieda turned her back, leaving me alone with my sister's face. With no recourse I grabbed the expensive scissors I had. They were given to me by Miss Linda, my friend's mom. Linda was a teacher at Marco Botelo, she sort of took me in at the end, said she wanted me to have good scissors. I grabbed my fancy gifted shears — scissors that are meant only for cutting hair — and snipped the tip off the bottle, wincing as the plastic bent and gave under the pressure of the closing titanium blades. The tip of the bottle flew up into the air, landing with a puff on the pillow of Zenieda's perm. My sister started laughing again, trying to hold it in, her bony shoulders going up and down violently, small sniffles erupting from her nose.

"Stop it," I said.

Fuck you, mouthed my sister. We were so alike, me and my sister, both having to have the last *fuck you*. It was genetic, erupting from somewhere deep beyond the DNA of our nuclear family, before cults and sandals. Like if I reached into the bowels of our family bucket I would uncover some foul-mouthed atheistic forebearer, a big-nosed, curly-haired asshole from the 1800s who blasphemed for fun, dangling from the tip of our family tree.

"No, fuck you," I said to my sister in full voice, breaking the zone, Zenieda's model almost flying out her seat like a gun went off.

"Shhhhhhh!" said the model.

"Oh, fuck you!" I said, now unafraid. "Fuck you *and* you!"

My sister broke into a knee-slapping hoot.

"Fuck you too," I said, giving up.

I was convinced that it was over, this test. I'm not supposed to be doing this. I'm not supposed to be in rooms with overhead lights, biting my tongue when I want to scream *Fuck you*. Grade-grubbing for a piece of paper. The testing monitor was glaring at us, making little checks on her clipboard. Right as she was about to say something, right in the middle of the test, the monitors switched. One went to another classroom and the other one came into ours. It had something to do with fairness or anonymity, the switch. Either way.

I left my body when the new tester entered the room. It was Miss Linda, my dear Miss Linda. Now I would have a chance. Linda's moral compass was weak in regards to testing and she had no ethical problem in passing me despite my monumental unpreparedness. *Please, God*, I whispered.

"What?" said my sister, wicked loud.

"SHHHHHHHT!" said Zenieda, still with the plastic tip dangling in her hair.

I smiled, rubbing my middle finger against my nose as Miss Linda made her way to my station. I couldn't have been luckier. I was holding my fancy scissors, the ones she gave me, to my sister's head, doing a mock haircut. Linda was my Golden Ticket.

"What the hell happened to you?" Linda said. I had forgotten about the garage pit, forgotten I was hemorrhaging all over my white pressy pants. Stupid white pants, they finally looked cool, dark clots of blood fixing them to my legs. I had forgotten that I stunk like a wino, that I was still drunk. *You're totally drunk*, my sister had said when I picked her up. *Loser*, she said, *pull it together*. Four hours ago I was stumbling around my house trying to find a blowdryer that worked. Now here I was with a room full of talent, trying to hold all my blood in.

"I fell in a garage pit," I told Linda.

"A what?"

"A hole," my sister said. "Dumbass went and fell in a hole."

"This morning?"

"Last night," I said, trying to keep my death-breath away from her perimeter.

Linda grabbed a few strands of my sister's hair, in the area where we had to cut at least a half an inch off. The variations in length were outrageous. Where it should have been a solid line of layers were giant gaps, Miss Linda's eyes filling the holes and rolling. She was horrified. She looked at me through my sister's messed-up hairline and ripped me a new one with her arching brows. Now even my Golden Ticket was looking like it may not come through. She wouldn't even look at me after the test was over.

At the end I passed real slow behind Linda's desk and over to the sink to fake-wash my hands and to look over her shoulder. Miss Linda grabbed a giant red pen out of the desk canister in its crocheted cozy. Oh, god, no, not red ink. My friend Bidhya once told me that in India you never ever write in red ink unless it's bad news or a past-due bill or something.

Linda took the hostile red ink and pulled it across a cube of notepaper. I didn't want to see the word FAIL. I peeked through my closed lashes and saw it, a bright red 71 bleeding into the top of an orange post-it. When she was sure I was looking, she put a big circle around the number, letting me know I had passed the test. If it wasn't so illegal, what she did, I would have hugged her right there, jumping up and down. I wanted to know how Zenieda did.

"I hope you got a zero, Zenieda." I threw my shit into a bag and let my sister figure out the way to the car. I had done it. I was now a licensed cosmetologist.

My first job out of Marco Botelo, before I moved on to New York and San Francisco, was at Mark James Salon Systems in Providence. The title "Salon Systems" would indicate that there were several locations but there was just the one on Power Street. A glossy black salon wrapped in huge windows, it was very high-end. I was lucky to get the apprenticeship. Mark James ripped his business model from NYC's John Demonte, who I would come to work for later in my career. The hairdresser's hairdresser, John Demonte, is still the only person I name when asked who taught me anything. Him and Miss Linda. I love John Demonte.

Mark James was no John Demonte; he was the opposite of all things Demonte. Mark James was a big old queen and we all knew it, no matter how many people attended his wedding. He married Trisha, who had been his blonde beard since high school. Even with their new baby beard, Mark James seemed to me like a faggot of the highest order with all the worst stereotypes attached. Prone to pitching fits, with a wavy golden brown tousle just so at his forehead, Mark was a mean bitch. It was a closet-case situation, and like any situation, I'd imagine it was only made worse by the arrival of a baby.

Trisha, referred to as "Trasha" by the staff, would prance into the salon daily holding their red-faced, screaming ball of hate. The baby smelled like Nanny hugs. Trasha seemed beyond over the baby at all times. When holding it or pushing it in a stroller, she would eye-roll whenever it made a noise. It was a show cat of a child, wrapped in Hermes.

I never bothered to remember its name, gender, or eye color, too put-off by its bright pink screams and wrestling hands, pushing hard on its mother's chest, *away*, *away*. As soon as I saw it being rolled in I'd check out, only looking when it was wrapped in a new scarf. I would have killed that puddle of screams for just one of its designer outfits, had I been an adjacent infant with my adult brain.

In the Salon, the baby's dad either hated me or wanted to fuck me, I couldn't tell, but so gross either way. Mark would stand over me as I washed towels, a bump in the front of his khaki slacks, *khaki* being a word that would make my sister and me erupt into laughter whenever we heard it. "Do you need to make a khaki?" my sister would ask. "Khaaaa-keeeee!" We would laugh so hard then, but now — now that my boss was pushing his khaki into my elbow while I shampooed his wife — it wasn't funny at all.

In my experience, there's something wrong with hetero hairdressers. It's just not right. Maybe that's why I was sure that Mark James was a homo. No straight men got their hair cut by Mark. A salon that's all black lacquer and glass picked out by a hetero doesn't add up.

My uniform for Mark James was basic black until I *got on the floor* in a year, when I would graduate to a black and white color palette. No flair. I always felt uncomfortable at any job — but hairstyling is a job where people have expectations coming in. Nobody wants to go to a stylist who has hair that looks like it is rotting as it grows, with bad nose and ear hair issues. I get that. But then it goes further, where nobody wants to go to a stylist that isn't stylish in appearance. The client wants a complete look.

If you're a lady, you need to bring to the floor long, stretchy bellbottoms over impossible heels with a white top. For a man, a t-shirt tucked into a pair of new black designer jeans will work, if you have the body for it. Otherwise you can do the giant poet shirt and black shorts with black leggings and buckle shoes — pilgrim — and work that angle. I was never good at this costuming. I wear the same thing every day and can never find an outfit that connects The Industry with how I feel inside. Unable to find a middle ground between gutter scum and platform artist, I find myself at Ross Dress for Less buying another pair of horrid slacks and a black shirt.

Clothes always look good at Ross. Everything does. The combination of the price tag and the need to get out of the store has forced me to make purchases I would never make if I knew any better or cared. That's the thing. I don't care. At all. I can do your hair and make you look like anything you want, I can transform you, but how's about me? Why do I have to wear a monkey suit to do my job?

My first week at Mark James Salon Systems I had to bring in a model to do a full head of foil highlights, to show my proficiency. My big mistake was to bring my sister, my State Board test model sister, with her Roseanne Roseannadanna hair and her inability to not make fun of me. Mark James instructed me on his method of doing foils, which was a stupid, bumbling technique in hindsight, and then let me go at it when my sister came in at 11. Just like at my State Board test, my sister could not have been more trouble.

"What's up, Dicknose?" she said when I came to collect her in the waiting area. "Nice pants." It took four hours for me to weed through my sister's hair while my family convened at the Spaghetti Warehouse to wait on the results. She fussed through the whole process, making khaki jokes, and laughing at how my pants whistled when I walked.

Mixing up bucket after bucket of hair-eating bleach, I kept throwing the foils in, hoping it would push past orange. Using Mark's ridiculous system of neat folds I was all thumbs, smears of bleach burning red circles into my sister's forehead.

"What the fuck, Francis?"

"Shut up, I'll fix it."

"Wipe it!" My sister started screeching, the whole of the salon looking over. "Wipe it, Francis, it's in my eye!" Mark James swished up in his khakis, a big bustle of panic. "Aaaagh! Wipe it! Aaaaaaaghhhhh!"

"She's over-reacting," I told Mark.

"You should get her to the sink," he said, my sister getting louder.

I dragged her from the chair over to the shampoo bowl, huge globs of foil dropping with dull thumps on the tile with every step. I could see orange streaks painted into the fabric of her hair.

"Flush my eyes! Flush my eyes!" I had the hose pressed up against her face, blasting cold water into her eyes. "Keep flushing them, Francis! Aagghhhh!"

"I am! Shut up… I'm gonna get in trouble."

"Fuck you, *shut up*! You shut up! You're a clown, Francis, a real fuckin' clown. Rinse it out! Rinse it out and let me outta here!" Those were the last words my sister spoke to me that night. After seeing the results from under the towel she was speechless. Orange strings like French fries hung in masses of cotton candy damage, me trying to cover it all up with what was left of her natural hair.

"It looks okay if you flip it like this," I said, trying to show her how to cover the carnage but she wasn't having it. No words, only imminent tears.

"How's it going over here?" Mark's moon face filled the mirror between my sister's cloud and mine.

"Oh, fine. I'm just gonna get her dried and we're gonna go." My sister burst into tears, fried ends crumpling in her fingers. Mark walked into the back with Trasha, both of them freaking out in the office at the mess I made of my sister's head.

"Don't pull at it," I said, getting her dried and out the door. "Let's go eat."

When we walked into the Spaghetti Warehouse, my family, along with most of the restaurant — which is giant, it's a warehouse — went silent. My sister had taken the bandana she had dangling from the rearview of her car and tied it around her head as a scarf.

Giant curls of orange poked out the sides, making her look like some dangerous hobo woman. The waitress looked like she wanted to cry when she came over, like maybe she had a shitty hairdresser brother, too. I ordered water, my sister ordered the Bottomless Rigatoni, and nobody in my family has ever let me touch their hair again.

II

The analysis of scalps has become the basis of my new theory, an offshoot of Phrenology, the study of the skull made infamous by Dr. Joseph Gall and his fellow anatomists in the 1800s. My theory goes deeper, ignoring the shape of the skull and the flippant stereotyping that goes along with it. Phrenologists looked at the book and never the cover. It's too bad; they were so close.

While peeling back the skin of cadavers to get a closer look at the bone structure of the cranium — its bumps, notches and minute variations — they erased the very information they were seeking. While running his hands over the heads of the nobles, becoming a glorified fortune teller for the jet set of the day, Dr. Gall overlooked the solution: that the answers lie in the scalp itself.

The condition of that layer of skin, coating all of those cranial bumps, offers specifics the bumps themselves cannot. That skin, so fascinating in its supple tension; the incredible density of blood vessels waiting below its surface, waiting to spurt with one quick slip of my shears, it can sing. From the front hairline, over the parietal ridge and to the base of the occipital protuberance, the scalp holds in the secrets of the brain within. Secrets thin enough to slip through bone. When the room starts spinning and the secrets come out, I want to slice scalp clean off with my straight razor. I want to expose their transgressions to the world. I want to free them.

Instead I chew my lip as I scrub their scalps, massaging their containers until they drift off. As the clear water runs through the filth of their hair I whisper a silent prayer to bring another day of serving others to an end, praying that nobody fills me with psychic pain as they sit in my chair. There isn't enough time to process it, all that pain. I always finish up as fast as I can before a new demon walks in requesting a wash and set.

People tell me everything. Without prodding or consent, clients go quickly past the white lie of a few foil highlights straight to the guts of their inner demons. The secrets of marital infidelity. The secrets of alcoholism, of abuse, of murder. While their confessions are no more than blathering fantasy pouring from the mouths of pathological liars, I prefer to take their stories as truth, to be both polite and entertained. Only her hairdresser knows for sure. No shit.

The contact made its origin at the fare-box of the 22 Fillmore bus, snaking around briefcases and wheelchairs until it reached the center back seat of the bus, where I sat. A screaming HELLO! from her retinas to mine. She smiled at me as I forced my eyes to my feet and my shoulders threw themselves at each other. She was about to start waving. I have no idea who she is, let alone assign her a name, but I am sure that I have touched her scalp before. I pretend to be immersed in a *Watchtower* picked up off the rubber mat of the bus floor. She continued gesturing. I unfocused my vision, wrapping myself in a shield of metallic green, its filter pulled as close and tight as scuba skin.

My fingertips have caressed her scalp, I'm betting, maybe only once while I cut her hair and took her money. Maybe it was ten times. Her cut hair, like everyone else's, was swept up and placed in the box labeled A Matter Of Trust from which it would be sent off to make mats for absorbing oil spills. The crinkled bills that she paid me were smoothed and folded, little squares placed into the bottle near my bed, the bottle marked WEALTH. These small details I remember: her hair, shorn and collected, went on to do great things for the environment, just as sure as my hungry hands removed several dollars from my wealth jar every morning like clockwork. But her name, it was gone ten minutes after her hair was dry.

Names and faces, they disappear faster than they come in. Kathy, Susan, Barbara — they all blend into one faceless skull. I remind myself that name recall is only crucial while they are sitting in my cutting chair, that only when I am touching them do I need to remember them. When they leave they take their names with them, closing the salon door as my hands twitch above the next client's head. If only my hands could remember what my brain blocks out after contact with the scalp is broken.

On the bus it's easy to pretend not to see them, with the option of jumping off at the next stop should they ignore my cry to be left alone in my green shield. In the salon I have to keep my clients visible at all times because they pay me to stay focused. They pay to feed on me.

What's-her-face on the bus seemed nice enough and I appreciate her keeping her distance. She didn't push it. I still don't remember her but I'd wager she had one squeaky-clean scalp, what with all the smiling she does. It works that way. Nice people/good tippers have nice clean scalps while most miserable assholes/bad tippers have some sort of scalp disorder — scabs that ooze pus, abrasions, infected follicles, or at least some waxy yellow flakage. The intensity of the disorder is relative to the level of whatever -ism the client presents with upon first leaning their vile heads into my shampoo bowl.

Squeaky-clean didn't get off at the same stop as I did, allowing me a peaceful walk through Mission's morning, my thoughts unseen by all forms of Satanic passersby. Free to enjoy head space is rare in this place, in San Francisco, a city so electric with wires and pops firing just above your head. Just a little too close. New York City is fed from below, from subways and the hollowed-out spaces beneath the visible. San Francisco pushes in pulsating zaps that connect with the pavement, vibrating. I'll follow these wires up Market and down Church, back up 16th to Mission. The positive and negative charges swirl around my face and pull me in zigzag down Mission. I have to keep reminding myself to move my feet or I'll just be stuck there with everyone else, waiting for morning to scream from its cuntface lair; faces upturned to pink fog and descending planets.

All these things you hear people talking about, you notice it when you end up here. Things that go into retrograde or line up in convergence. You start to believe it when you live here for a while. When the pops from the wires make your head turn up and wait, the realization that the planets are lined up to dry-fuck you seems to explain everything cleanly.

When I walk in New York, I look down. The energy hovers low, like a blanket to protect the saints, and the rumble of the subway feeds the soles of a million kinds of shoes. For now, I'm pretty sure I'm walking down streets in the Mission. They feel spongy. These Mission streets look different every second of every day. Asphalt morphs into rippling waves that chew, digest, and expel constantly, their tiny razor teeth hidden beneath a blue lip of water and foam, only jabbing in to rip muscle after washing gently over trusting skin.

San Francisco energy is forcing down hard today. You know a zap is coming but you don't know when, like when the eye doctor gives you the glaucoma air puff test, a heavy burst of pressurized air against the eyeball, and he says, "Relax." How to relax when a blast of air is about to reset my eye in its socket is beyond me but the doctor always says it and I flinch every time. Same with a chiropractor. *Relax. Relax while I snap your neck violently to the side.*

To counteract any forming scalp obsession I think about my shoes stolen from Worn Out West, the overpriced used denim/leather store on Castro. When I look in adoration at the tips of them as I walk, I don't regret the risk of stealing them. It was so easy. The old trick. After removing the pathetic sneakers that I had worn into the store, I slid on the heavy Red Wing boots and slipped out of the store before the cashier could take notice. He was busy sorting used cockrings and butt plugs for resale, a job that must be difficult as a buyer. "This one here's a little too worn in, I'm not gonna take this one," he'd have to say.

The boots that I liberated have a small heel so I worried they looked faggy but once I had them on, I could tell they were mine. Already broken in, my boots had seen years of use in the bars south of Market Street, wrapping their leather around a weekend warrior who spun under spotlight on their steel-toed tips. I picture the queen throwing glitter around heartlessly as he spins.

Talk to me about a bar and I'll talk to you about glitter. Glitter ruins everything and should be banned. One careless toss of the hand by a glitter queen and two weeks later you find sparkles like prisms on your toilet paper. You hope to God that the glitter was on the paper before you wiped but you know better. Don't ask yourself how the lone piece of glitter got lodged in your butthole, just wipe again and flush, reminding yourself that it gets everywhere. It just does.

The soles of my boots, erased of their glittery past, go well with my uniform this month and are the only item that I can call my own. The black shirt with the red snake on it is Roxanna's. The socks and jeans are Sluggs. The bright blue cardigan came from Colleen All-Cars, a special gift that I sport every day, making the dealers call me Cookie Monster. The day she gave me the sweater was the day that I realized palm trees grew on Mission Street. Big old ones. All that time walking with my head down, shielded from the electric attack from above, it never occurred to me that such beauty could be my canopy.

An organization set up a food table outside a BART station, offering sandwiches and literature and enlightenment. One of the lesser demons singles me out and tries to hand me a leaflet, which I refuse and walk on. Each footstep calls upon a different Saint for protection, and with each intercession my green filter expands a bit further until small amounts of sunshine are allowed to permeate my shield and reach my skin. An orb of chartreuse floats me down the scraped pavement, holding me as I lean forward in daytime walking trance. As I observe what is real from behind the veins of this bubble, the Agents of Darkness turn invisible and lotus blossoms drip honey onto my head.

Here in the waiting room of the free clinic where I see Jherri, my therapist, I make plans I never carry out. Plans of bloodletting and of leeches sucking flesh. I tell nobody about these ancient thoughts, not even Jherri. Especially not Jherri. Never tell a therapist anything that could expose you later.

Looking around at the skulls that rest atop the other bodies in the waiting room, I regret that I can't lay my hands on them before Jherri comes and calls me into her teeny office. Like Kathryn Kurden, I want to make the waiting room tremble and fall out, unknown languages passing their tongues as their bodies hit the checkerboard. With a firm shampoo I could help these people more than Jherri ever could. All she can do is pass out advice. When I am Hairdresser, I try to not pass out advice. It's too much responsibility. If my job was giving advice, I would give bad advice.

Jherri spent her Ivy League years toiling to earn a master's, an overblown degree that would allow her only to hand out lukewarm advice, never good or bad. And she can't even write prescriptions. What a waste. To become a hairdresser I learned my own brand of psychology with the help of Miss Clairol. While I have sometimes scored Valium and weed for my clients, many of my clients give me drugs for doing such a meticulous job on their hair. Win/win. I'm glad I took the trade.

Jherri is taking forever today. She likes to make us wait until her outline appears behind the frosted glass that leads past reception. She stops and engages the receptionist with small talk.

"Bad case of the Mondays, Tammy?"

Tammy looks at Jherri with a *hold-on-a-second*, holding her index finger two inches from Jherri's nose. Shushing her softly. *Good one, Tammy*. In the waiting room we listen, wondering who Jherri will call in first. There's no order, no list of names. Hal catches my eye from across the floor and lets out an extended sigh. A groan. An *ugh*.

Jherri stays by Tammy, waiting for the shushing finger to drop but Tammy won't look up, running her free hand across the useless appointment book. She does this every time Jherri comes to collect a kook from the cast of characters lining the walls. Tammy's ruse always comes off as believable. She truly looks busy.

"We'll catch up later, Tammy, you busybody!" Jherri says, waving her hands to say *for the life of me I have no idea how Tammy gets it all done*, ten exclamation points trailing her. Crossing from behind the glass, she bellows into the waiting room, "Frank, I can see you now."

"Ugh," we all say in unison; me because she called my name first, the rest of them because she didn't. "Ugggghhh." It's natural for us who sit and wait to say *ugh*. A slow, controlled release of breath from those of us who never exhale, an accidental yogic practice generated by the anxiety that is held by certain rooms. We sit, silent in these rooms, until we can't hold it in anymore. We clutch the air in our lungs until something forces us to breathe out, a collective *uuuggh* breaking the psychic tension of the room. We, the people who wait in lines and small rooms, we use "Ugh" the way Buddhists use "Om."

"Frank, I can see you now," Jherri says.

"Francis," I say. "Like the Saint. Saint Francis."

"Walk this way, Frank," she says, setting me up for the oldest joke in the book, a bit of vaudeville from way back. Like Mel Brooks, I mimic her heady walk behind her back as she passes through the waiting room, raising groans from my audience. I have to do it. I can't help it; my life is a teevee dramatic comedy and if I stop acting it will end.

The murmur of the waiting room muffles when Jherri closes the balsa wood door of her office but I can still hear them *ugh*ing in response to my exit performance. She is unable to maneuver around the artificial ficus tree and get to her seat before I launch into my sales pitch for Scalp

Phrenology. It's all I really have for her this visit.

"Jherri, while I was sitting in the waiting room, I couldn't help but notice the shape that old Hal's scalp is in. It's practically falling off in chunks, for chrissakes! You notice?" *You notice*, I ask, as if the whole world makes a habit of follicle analysis. "I mean I can see bad tippers deserving dry scalp, but HAL?" I'm waiting for Jherri to come up with a response, an "Oh my GOD, I know, right?!" sort of thing but I get nothing. Typical.

"Maybe it's a different type of flaking. I'd have to touch it. There must be some way to connect specific scalp disorders with different states of guilt and misery..." I'm looking at the wall as I talk. Jherri could be in the bathroom for all I know. When I check, she is still there in her expensive chair, sitting with no comment. She couldn't care less and lets me go on.

"Greedy people have a certain type of flakage that will never, ever go away. No shampoo can scrub away the filth of capitalism, Jherri. No conditioner to soften the coarse bristles of missed deadlines and enraged overseers. Bad people have bad scalps and I see a lot of bad people daily. Many of them just have the beginnings of a serious disorder. Dry scalp, itching. The stuff you see on commercials. No big whoop, you think, right? But I mean they're young still, Jherri! Seventeen, eighteen. With itching and flaking. Already. And they obsess on it, making everything worse. They ask me, 'My scalp is so dry it cracks, can you recommend anything?' I mean, what do I say, Jherri? What would you say?"

Jherri says, "Maybe we should talk about you. What do you think?"

"This is about me, Jherri!" She's not getting it at all. Jherri's got a flaky yet somehow waxy scalp, a disorder I haven't figured out yet but believe to be some sort of fungal bipolarity.

"Look, Jherri, most clients would never understand the concept of the New Phrenology, so I just tell them 'anything you can buy at the drugstore is just as good as what you can buy in some fancy salon...' I mean, why make them spend money when none of it will work anyway?"

"So true..." Jherri makes a note in my file: BUY WHAT'S ON

SALE.

"They're flaky, dry, and scabby on the inside and it's forcing its way out through the blood vessels and follicles of the scalp. Their shame is the culprit, causing the sores and pustules to worsen."

"Eww," Jherri says, breaking protocol before quickly backpedaling. "I mean, that must be difficult with your panic and everything. How is that going, Frank, the panic?"

"Oh God, Jherri, the panic! Sometimes the energy emanating from a scalp is enough to make me recoil, rolling back on my heels as soon as I touch it. Almost audible, the pain of a bad day, you know how that goes, Jherri. But touching people is different, Jherri, harder. For suspended seconds, I drag my hands along the recesses of a person's temples, getting a glimpse of their day's misery. Sometimes I see further, if they let me in. They have to let me in. They have to turn and face the itching."

I shift in my seat at the thought of itching. The mention of mites and lice always makes me itchy from the inside out. The bones in my hands try to push out through my fingertips when I stretch and yawn in the red plastic seat in front of Jherri's desk.

Jherri touches her mid-length bob, a study in exactitude a la Vidal Sassoon circa 1982. She has that one haircut, the Type-A with the back raised up in strict geometry and severe lines all the way around, her bangs framing her face with surgical precision.

"Do you find that working with people helps or hinders your ability to deal with your panic?" Jherri doesn't want to talk hair anymore. She's wondering if her bob is all in place. (It is, but the ends are thirsty and need a good conditioner.)

"Jherri, I don't just cut their hair. They tell me everything in hideous detail, thinking that my lips are sealed when they leave. They don't realize that there are no laws regarding hairdresser/patient confidentiality."

Jherri bristles when I compare what I do to what she does. Her Master's hangs on the beige wall behind her, next to a posterboard that says "DISCOVER THE FUN OF SUMMER!!!" across the top, pictures of shiny nuclear families having picnics burst from glitter-glued stars. Jherri made the poster, I can tell by the loopy letters. I should probably go.

Jherri isn't writing anything anymore, just sitting there thinking about the itch at the base of her cranium and how she would jab at it with her blue pen as soon as I left. Picking up on my flight response, Jherri hits me with "What made you get into hairdressing in the first place?" She looks into her notepad and says, "You don't have to answer that. Just think about it."

She's not kidding either. Handing out this mental homework filled with questions that don't need to be answered. From the face she put on as she asked the question you'd have thought we were talking about racial cleansing or infanticide, not hairdressing. Jherri's bob appeared more severe than ever as she got dead serious: "Just think about it, Frank. Time's up."

As I squash back into the waiting room Jherri yells from her desk, "And SMILE, Frank."

Before the assembled group could groan a prayer, right before I thought she was going to say, "Turn that frown upside down," she switched it up and said, with a straight face, "Just smile, Francis...and fake it till you make it...," and then she added, "A phony smile is better than a real frown."

A phony smile is better than a real frown. Did she make that up? She had to. Or if she heard it, she must believe it if she advocates it. Old Hal in the waiting room is almost always smiling, usually without engaging his eye muscles, just showing his teeth. Just a-smilin' like a mongoloid, smiling like a chimpanzee smiles when it is cornered and about to attack.

Miss May nods out in my chair. Watching her head fall forward, I hold it, grabbing at the brittle strands of hair near the base of her scalp so it doesn't hurt. It only hurts when you pull the hair against its natural growth pattern, so always pull down.

She's deep into the nod. I cough, clearing my throat loud enough so she realizes that she is somewhere. So she remembers she had left the house today. I don't want her to wake in an embarrassed startle, having no idea where she is or how she got there. I hate that feeling.

The day begins to come back to her in ripples, water in a lake wearing away at silt shoreline in continuous determined waves. Her bones adjust in the yellow plastic chair and her eyes pop open. I stand behind her, stroke her hair. It's fine, her hair, but she's got a lot of it.

"Hey, Cha-Cha, I'm losing more to the drain every time, the bastard, so make it puffy in back. Cover up that goddam bald spot. Puffy, honey." May calls me Cha-cha more often than she calls me Francis. It's all part of the movie we star in, layers of plots and sub-plots entertaining us for hours.

"I gotcha, honey. More puff for your stuff, huh, May?"

My co-workers resent May and me. Annoyed by their walk- on roles in our lives and sick to death of our repertoire, they push us out of their reality or try to shove themselves into ours. But we choose the plots and the players; we people the landscape. The other stylists are disposable, occurring only when we need a side character to toy with.

"Yes, puff that stuff till you can't get enough," she says, coughing a laugh into a napkin. "Damn bald spot gets bigger every day, that's for sure, more skin, less hair. The puff'll cover it up. Whadda they call that? A brush-down?"

"A comb-over?"

"Yeah, that's it, Chach, a comb-down. Make me look like Donald Trump."

May asks about balding two, three times a visit so I have a system to calm her. I measure the spot with a coin, holding a nickel up to her scalp. When I first met May it was the size of a dime, the bald spot. Now it's a bit smaller than a nickel.

"You sure you're not measuring with a quarter up there, Cha-Cha? Or one of these Sacagawea's they give you at the bank? Goddamn things. I always use 'em like quarters on accident. It's a coup, I tell ya. I think the little teller girl at the pull-up only gives them to me. Then that little guy at Walgreens, the slow one, he orders lipsticks for me, acts real sweet. I pay, you'd think he'd say, 'Hey old lady, that's a Sacagawea you gave me instead of a quarter,' but no, he pockets the seventy-five cents off the dollar. It's a coup, I say. For seventy-five cents. Goddamn Sacagawea."

I love when the heat rises and May rages against the injustice that is daily life. People think she's just ranting, a crazy old lady yakking away. They pin the label of Crazy to her skin, thinking *well, she must be crazy, right, Francis? I mean, is she just nuts or what*?

She's a genius comedienne to me, brilliant and on top of it, even for all the meds she takes. She's a pro: when the pharmaceutical mix gets heavy, May doesn't slur her words or stumble around. When she's confused, she closes her eyes and stops talking. She's never sloppy. And she's not crazy. *Crazy* is one of the worst things people can throw around. We're all crazy. May is no different, but her age makes her an automatic target for the name callers. She's *crazy*, she's *mean*, she's *crotchety*, and she's *losing it*, they say.

Most of the pills she takes are for pain, some are for anxiety. Some of them are there to counteract the prickly brain waves induced by the first round of pills. She takes big ones, small ones, and those little pink footballs that make you forget things in the middle of a sentence. That's when she stops talking.

The pills I take for my panic — the pills that went on to replace heroin — are yellow rectangles with lines scored into them so you can split them into four but I don't do that. Plugging up pinprick holes in my brain's frontal lobe, the rectangles put hospital corners over emotions and tuck them in for the night. Magic Pills, so tiny like crumbles, they absorb the moment between when the paper slices the side of your finger, and when the slice begins to burn and bleed. At the precipice of the paper cut and its stinging manifestation, that's where the rectangles hold me.

I'm always wondering when I'm going to start to bleed out my nose or mouth. That's what the pills are for, so I don't have to think about bleeding or paper cuts or earthquakes. There are other things that I should care about like bills and rent but most of that time I'm thinking *where the fuck are my rectangles?* or I'm waiting for an aneurism to hit.

May's been taking the meds for years, to the point where everything's leveled off and all of the pain is equalized in her brain. The Sacagawea's piss her off as much as the price of her prescriptions; the plight of African orphans gets under her skin to the same degree as public displays of affection.

"I stopped picking my battles thirty years ago. Now all I can do is keep my gun at my hip, safety off, just in case," she says. "Locked and loaded." I suspect she does have a gun at her hip, hidden under the blue shampoo cape. "I guess they need it more than I do, the seventy-five cents. People are starving out there, Cha-Cha, what can you do? Maybe the slow gal doesn't realize it either and her fat-cat manager pockets it at the end of her shift. Stupid Sacagawea."

"It's *not* a Sacagawea." I show her the nickel before placing against her scalp, a magician showing a top hat to the audience. "Look, look, look, it's the same as last time, May. A nickel. Even smaller than a nickel. Remember that your hair is fine but dense. I see this hair every week, Maybelline, so I, not Sacagawea, would know best if it were dropping out. Right?"

"Fine but dense, my skinny white ass... Christ, Francis, I'm gonna end up looking like goddamn Don Rickles if I keep listening to you."

May is dressed in her favorite tropical sundress. She always dresses for the beach. Even in the wettest of San Francisco winters she's all flower prints and spaghetti straps.

"The Hello Gorgeous Beauty Salon, 17th Street, San Francisco," May says out loud, doing a little drum roll on the arms of the chair.

"Yes, ma'am. And I must indicate that your hair is shining, just like the sun, Miss May. Now you rest your eyes, lovely lady, let me work my magic. She loves this over-the-top service, when the hair and its jargon reach levels of satire. She knows I don't work magic with hair. She doesn't come for the hair. The usual forced conversations between the server and the served fall away as I rub her shoulders, a level of closeness I allow only with May.

With other clients, I make a constant effort to keep the acting up to par and really turn it out. With coddling interest I discuss politics, listen to stories of torn marriages and trips to Cancun, all while feigning complete understanding. I never have any idea what they're talking about but the general idea is that most people hate their jobs, their partners, and their lives far more than they hate the texture of their hair.

I loathe touching them and spend most of my day psychically shielding myself from their misery. Usually I will shield in the morning, allowing me to successfully battle Satan on my way to work. He stands on every corner, sits next to me on the bus. He offers me spare change even though I haven't asked for any. That's how I recognize Satan: he likes to help.

Psychic shielding is a simple ritual, one that I've always worked into the chaos of my mornings. I've made a few adjustments to suit my needs and have found it to be a satisfactory form of protection from the constant attack of Satan's minions, who surround me. Parish priests, bankers, the pig vice cops whose mission it is to set me up, people who smile on the bus — the agents of darkness are everywhere.

In a meditative state, I start at the tips of my toes and work my way up. My psychic shield is green feet pajamas. It's a green that only exists in mind. That *new* green. Made of a yet undiscovered metal, my feet pajamas can expand and contract, acting as a filter. In the moments where I'm comfortable, my shield is a wide bubble, allowing for interaction with outsiders. When confronted, I suck the suit close to my body, tight as scuba skin.

Walking from the bus stop, my filter is kept tight, providing enhanced immunity from the demons that corner me. Increased levels of psychic attack begin at the entrance to the salon. Insecurity and misery have a molecular weight lighter than air; they clutch the ceiling before forcing down on me by the blast of the Salon's central air.

"Francis, my hair is FRIED. I did it last night. *Feel it.* Fried, right? What are you going to do about it? I *hate* it. You have to get me in to-DAY or I'll die." The first person of the day always approaches with the elegance of a mad cow. Most clients are that way. Parasitic gnats, returning after each swat. Not with me. They try their hardest but their whining bounces off my green metallic skin and blends with the sound of blowdryers before it can assault my ears undiluted.

With Miss May I keep my pajama shield permeable. Verbal communication becomes secondary to psychic union when May sits, and we allow our shields to melt together to form a solitary bubble of safety. It's her, me, and the mirror. Where others fight the visions of the mirror, only seeing a reflection of what's visible, May opens the floodgates.

Jherri cuts all her hair off. Sans a bob, it's difficult recognizing her through the frosted glass. No sharp lines, just a stubbly round head that looks like freedom. I'm so proud of her. Such a breakthrough. After all these years, finally something. She had worn the geometry of her previous cut into the ground. It was her look, goddammit, and she wore it out.

The quarter-inch of buzz pushing from her follicles made me feel filthy by comparison, my curls untended and growing long, three inches of frizz encircling my face. My hair's in that middle place where it needs to turn a corner. That's what happens when you grow your hair out. It looks good for a few days at a certain length until it goes through another shitty phase. Then it turns a corner, overnight.

"Do you like it?" Jherri says, her question stuck in the air. "You don't like it."

When I look across at her head all I see is round. I like it, the giant round-head look, but it disarms me. By next week I'll get used to it, as will Jherri, but for now it's throwing us both off. Sitting with this altered version of Jherri, I'm dealing with a brand new therapist, fresh nerves shooting from both sides of the desk. I wonder what Tammy the receptionist thinks, what her reaction was when she unlocked the back door. Tammy hates change. And she hates Jherri, so the haircut, at best, would have garnered a lukewarm response.

Jerri's still in a place of shock. When you're so used to carrying one look, it begins to define you like a tattoo, and cutting it all off ushers in a few days regret.

"Do you like it though? You don't."

"Jherri, every time I shave my head I hate it for a few days but then it turns awesome. Don't worry," I say. She never said she was worried but now she is, trying to decipher what I meant by it *turns awesome*. I feel sad looking at the white line of scalp edging her tanned face, like a mismatched bald cap, one of the cheapo ones from Spencer's. I know the mania of hair clippers, how they feel in your hand, how they sing. It's easy to be pulled into the potential gratification of being shorn and thinking it will fix your life.

And I know the depression that follows the clipper song, when you look at the regret misting like spirits from the piles of hair that clog the sink. Single curls appear on creased jackets weeks after the cut, reminders of lengths past exhibiting strand by strand on pillowcases. Hair looks twice as long once it hits the floor, no matter how much you wanted off coming in.

"It's always a shock, Jherri." I should drop it but her head won't stop, sitting there on her neck. "It looks great on you, Jherri, it really does." I'm not lying. In two days, with a little stubble it will look fantastic. She exhales like a yogi. That's all she wanted to hear: it looks great on you. Now able to move on, she starts to take the papers out of my file and I notice how hairy her knuckles are.

"How are things at the salon, Francis?"

"Does it feel weird?" I say.

"What? Does what feel weird?"

"The wind on your head. Does it feel weird?"

Jherri is bummed that I haven't dropped the hair issue but I'm not the one who brought it to the table. I'm not the one who showed up bearing a radical new hair development. And even if it was my head, I would never ask someone if they liked it in the first place; it's a stupid question. And now, with Jherri, there's only 45 minutes left to reply. "It always feels weird to me to get that first wind on my scalp after I shave it, Jherri. It's intense. I've seen people pass out from it."

"Pass out? From getting a haircut?" Her smirk, now more pronounced against the backdrop of a fleshy head, gets tighter. Her smirk is her tell. Jherri thinks I'm lying.

"Yes, Jherri… it's not, like, commonplace or anything but, yeah, I saw it once when I worked for Demonte. I'm telling you, it really can happen." I made sure to keep my hands away from my mouth and my arms uncrossed while trying to connect eyes, doing all these things to show that I'm not making things up. I'd hate to get busted based on some small "liar's tic" that Jherri learned about in a seminar. Why would I lie about something so stupid? (This turns out to be a loaded question posited by my own brain, a question that causes me to stop and think, disabling my straight-shooter posture for something more tucked in at the heart.)

"You can pass out from it, Jherri… trust… the lady that passed out, she came in to get four feet cut off her hair…"

"Four FEET?" She picked up her pen. "Four feet," she repeated without the question mark, and wrote something in my file. Probably wrote *Francis is a fucking liar*. To make her see I wasn't lying I leaned forward in my chair, palms upward. I hadn't been to any seminars on this approach, but I had seen a few teevee shows, enough to know what The Man looks for during questioning.

"Yep. Four feet. She had been coming in for years and always got just a trim. It grew halfway from knee to ankle by the time she to cut it off."

"What made her cut it?" Light bounced off Jherri's shiny scalp, little points of repentance dancing across the landscape.

"You'd better get some sunscreen," I say.

"What?"

"Sunscreen. For your scalp. It'll burn, and that sucks. But, yeah. People change their hair for all kinds of reasons… loneliness, depression, guilt, shame, dysphoria… or sometimes they just want a change. You never really know. With this lady, it made me sad because she wasn't ready to cut it."

"What made her cut it?" Here she goes again with the question. I guess she had to, I never answered it.

"Pressure."

"From her husband? Her husband wanted her to?"

"I don't know, I don't even know if she was married, but it's all around, pressure. Pressure from all around. She had come in with a hair magazine, things like *Cute Short Cuts: Fifty and Fabulous; Sassy Cuts For Your Age- That Are In; Your Long Hair Makes You Look Like A Witch.*" I spoke the titles in a different voice, in a mocking teenager's voice. I hate when people do that, talk out of their own voice to belittle something, but here I was doing it.

"Did she? Look like a witch, I mean…"

"No. Well, maybe. But she liked her look. She should have never looked at the rules."

"The rules?" Jherri puts her pen down.

"Yeah, the rules. You know, like you're not supposed to have long hair past fifty, or anything below the shoulders is for teenagers… shit like that. Sometimes the haircut you're getting is decided on by the stylist before your ass even hits the chair, Jherri. Like if you have this head shape, you get *this* cut. That head shape gets *that* cut. Long face, layers at the cheekbone. And how you go to, like, the department store and they tell you you're a *fall* or a *summer*, and then they whip out some fabric. Ever do that one?"

"Yes! I'm a spring! That's why I wear these pastels. I don't love them but they're supposed to look good. Do you think they look good? What are you? I bet you're an autumn."

"That's all smoke and mirrors, Jherri." It makes me so mad when people fall into the rules. Not mad at the people for falling in, just mad. I've been mad in this industry since the first day of Beauty School. Since before. Since Glitz Iz Hair.

"They tell you, you can do *this* but you can't do *that*. This cut, not that color. Total crap! It bugs me, Jherri, it always has. I mean, some of it's useful, like they always put it in shapes, which makes sense I guess. I never really thought of it but it's like wearing vertical stripes for a slimming effect. Horizontal stripes do the opposite, ya know? I guess that does work but it should never be a rule, ya know. Like if you have a round head, they'll tell you to never wear a short, cropped cut."

The roundness of Jherri's melon shot straight up at this last sentence, and looking at its shape I knew her skull couldn't be any rounder, her hair any shorter, or my statement any more ill-timed. Jherri's used to this with me, this spurting of thoughts before thinking. Every week, I manage to offend her with no room for backpedaling.

Now I've made her feel bad. Never my intention, yet I know that the rest of the session — my session — will be spent convincing Jherri that *Yes, your hair looks terrific* when the truth is I don't care about hair anymore: Jherri's hair, my hair, or anyone's. Caring about lengths and style decisions isn't in me; as a result, all of my clients leave with hair that is soaking wet, or maybe towel-dried. I don't curl, shape, or style their new cut. That's their job. I won't be with them every morning as they scrunch, flatten, or heat their hair to foolish temperatures. There is the part of my job that is to train them in how to do such things but it's a part of the job that never interested me. I'll talk politics all day long. Moisturizers, not so much.

"So that lady that passed out after her haircut," Jherri asks, "was she old?"

"Cold?"

"Old," Jherri repeats. "Was she old?"

"I didn't ask, Jherri. She wasn't a teenager, if that's what you mean."

"What did she do for a living?"

Jherri was digging. I get this line of questioning a lot. Working in SoHo, I gathered a bunch of celebrity clients. People always want to know who. The famous names are the ones that stop them short, opening up more questions: *Oh my God! I loved her in* _____*! Is she nice? What does she talk about? Did she tip you? Did you give her that one haircut, that one in the '90s?* No, I didn't invent The Rachel.

It's the lesser names that I care about, the actresses who were famous in their day, before computers and The Universal Face. Women who looked real, with real lines and crow's feet, who kept their hair how they wanted it, not how their agents wanted it, their own independence blacklisting them from gaining more acting work.

Locked out of their industry, some take straight jobs or begin hoarding animals. Some of them will teach classes and workshops in Los Angeles, scoring the occasional walk-on cat lady role on a teevee show. Some of them will turn out for awards shows, drunk and disorderly until being asked to leave. Escorted out. Nationally Enquired. Booted. Infamy is the final reach at fame, a certain settlement. If they don't remember me for my Oscar in the '70s, they'll have to remember me for being the lady who fell screaming out of her chair at last year's Golden Globes. More headlines. No press is bad press. And they think they have to suffer. Again.

I keep my mouth shut when asked about the celebrities I've touched. It's not like I'm this incredible hairdresser who loves doing the work. And Jherri's perception of celebrity is probably different than mine. Most people's perceptions are. They want me to fill them with Isabella Rossellinis and Lauren Huttons but I didn't care.

Maybe I would have cared if I'd worked on Tonya Harding or Heidi Fleiss or any of the women I would die to touch, but the other ones? They were just actresses. And the lady with the four feet of hair was just that. A lady with four feet of extra hair. I didn't ask what she did for a living. I never do despite years of opposite coaching: *Always find out the client's profession and adjust the desired cut to match their job.*

"She was just a lady, Jherri. I mean, she wasn't royalty or anything."

Jherri looked sad about that. I must be such a boring slot in her sliding-scale book.

"She probably passed out from the shock of it, the weight lifting off her head. She got tipsy and lightheaded, and she passed out. It happens, Jherri, I swear."

"So when you shave a man's head, he may pass out?" Jherri was trying to make this exciting, playing Debate Club. Really, who gave a shit?

"I don't have many male clients; they usually go to other people."

"Why? Are you not good at them?"

"No, I'm really good at men's cuts. Barbering is one of my favorite things. I think they go to the next place because I charge them the same price as I charge the women. Like, the person that shaved your head, how much it run ya?"

"Seventy-five dollars," Jherri said.

"Okay, now, had you been a man, it would have been thirty," I said. Hell, it may have even been free for the man; I could picture the stylist saying, *Oh, jeez, Roger, I only ran a clipper across your scalp! So easy! Took two minutes!* And when Roger insists on paying it's all *Okay, just give me twenty, Rog. You're SO funny! You get outta here, mister!*

"Thirty?"

"Yeah. Men's cuts are cheaper than women's cuts. Men's soap is cheaper than women's soap. You never noticed that, Jherri?"

"I guess not. I mean, I never thought of it."

"Well, think of it," I said, leaving Jherri the mental homework for once. "Or don't! Time's up!" I got up and walked out, leaving Jherri alone at her desk with her flesh-head. From her drawer she grabbed a bottle of shampoo, a shampoo she just paid forty bucks for because it contains Yak-Semen Anti-Frizzplex. In the picture of a cat on her desk she sees the outline of her new hairdo and knows that her scalp won't be getting frizzy any time soon.

"Fuck," she says, getting up from her desk. "Hey, Tammy, ya need some shampoo? It's got the Yak stuff in it. It's the Frizzplex."

Tammy's already in the alley, smoking a More.

Therapy doesn't help me at all with hairdressing. Talking to Jherri doesn't make it so I'm not terrified by the thought of an appointment book with my name on the cover, filling itself with clients who need everything I can't give. I don't have the capacity. By process of elimination, you have stumbled upon me: the least motivated hairdresser ever.

Taffy's coming in today. She comes in every two weeks to the hour. I never know what to expect so I freak when I see her name in my book again. She's only come a few times and I hope each time will be the last. Chris the receptionist always makes sure to remind me the day before so I can psychically prepare for what's about to happen.

"Hey, Francis! Taffy's here. She's here now!" He said it all in faggot code so I knew I was in for it. (We are an ancient people who have ways of communicating that go undetected to the heterosexual eye. We don't wait until you leave to begin talking about you; we do it right in front of you and you never even know it). In Fag-Latin, Chris's words, loosely translated, said: *Listen, girl, look. Taffy's here… do not look at her nose… tighten up, hun, because she looks in-sane… Watch out, Francis… keep the light.* Then he turned his back to me.

"Francis is ready for Taffy!" Chris screamed to the lobby.

"Thanks, Chris," the mother said, dragging Taffy across the room by her arm, gripped tight below the elbow. "C'mon, Taffy doll. Let's move! Aren't ya excited?"

"No."

"Yes, you are! You're *so* excited! Tell Francis you're so excited."

"I'm so excited," Taffy said in a tone equivalent to an eye roll.

As she sat I tried to not focus on her new nose but it's hard when the change is so drastic. Her nose had been done, but not like removing-a-deviated-septum done, like *done* done. Over. Done.

Someone put a scalpel about three-quarters an inch above the ball of Taffy's preteen nose and sliced clean from that point to where the nostrils connect, cutting off the tip. Sharper than a pig's nose, its new tip joined her face at a severe angle, the opposite angle of the short-to-long we see in an A-line bob.

"What can I do ya for, Taffy?" She's so small in my chair, filling up my station with all of her things. She has an iPod, an iPad, and an iPhone, all needing a charge.

"Can you plug this in? I mean, can I plug it in… my iPad? Is there a plug, Francis?"

"Of course, honey, let me just find an outlet… let me just unplug the blowdryer and I—"

"She doesn't need to plug it in," her mother says, grabbing the plug to my blowdryer out of my hand. "Taffy, you don't need to plug it in. Jeez. Always plugging something in, we can't go anywhere, Francis, not anywhere without this one having to use other people's electric." She points her thumb at Taffy and I wonder how often she calls Taffy *this one*.

Crouched under my station, she's tossed away the iPlug and is trying to plug my blowdryer back into its socket. She's got the plug backwards where the big tooth slot is on the wrong side but she just keeps jamming at the hole thinking it will stretch. "Fuckin' thing. Francis, how does it go in?"

"Flip it over."

She turns the blowdryer onto its head, considering what I had told her and figuring that the plug was going to fit now. It was that simple.

"No, the plug. Flip it…"

"What?"

"Flip the plug over."

"Flip the plug over? It's a plug, Francis, two prongs…"

"I know, but—"

"Flip it over…" she mutters from under the station.

I pull her out from under me, take the plug from her hand and flip in around, then crouch down and slide it into the socket — the big tine on the left side — it goes right in, even fits a little loose.

"There we go!" she claps, as if we had accomplished something together. The iPad lets out one final bleat before shutting itself down, and Taffy frowns. Taffy wants an A-Line bob but her mother won't allow it. "I don't think soooo, not yet… Taffy's too young for that. Don'tcha think, Francis? Too young?"

I never know what to say to Taffy's mother. She's an incident report waiting to happen.

"I mean she's got the face for the A-line… *finally*." She says *finally* from behind her hand like she's telling a dirty joke. "Right, Francis? She's got the face? The face for it? I mean, I like the A-Line *idea* on her, but still… let's not. Let's wait. At least until she's thirteen!" She snorkel-laughs and then catches herself. "Ahhh… but I just, ya know, I don't want her haircut to make her look old."

"She's twelve…"

"She's eleven! Don't rush her!" snorkel-laugh, composure. "But you know what I mean."

"I don't."

"Yes, you do! You *know*! You better know! That's your job, Francis!"

"Well, I mean, I guess I know."

"You totally know, you're just not listening."

Words like that make me want to kill. I have to shift my focus off the mother before I say something we'll all regret. "Taffy, what do you think?"

"She can't hear you." Her mother taps at the iPod. "Earphones… and don't ask her, anyways. She doesn't know anything. If it was up to her she'd be eating bugs and riding her brothers Big Wheel around the yard. Jesus Christ, she loves that thing. Just going in circles all day. Ahhh, what can ya do… ugh. I hate it. I was so different at her age, like *so* different. I always tell Taffy I think maybe the hospital gave me the wrong kid, the old switch-a-roo, ya know? But she has her father's eyes and weird head. The bastard. What was I thinking… it's just I had so many bad haircuts when I was Taffy's age, I don't want that to happen here… She has that weird neck, so be careful… you went a little too short last time."

People say that every time. *You went a little too short last time.* Go shorter, they say, and when I do it's too short and all my fault. I've stopped going shorter at all, just going through the motions of cutting, knowing they'll think it's too short no matter what. This placebo-cutting takes more time than real cutting, it's such a performance. But it's worth it to know that I've warped their perception with ten minutes of miming. Busy fingers and the click of scissors slicing air, the only thing missing is Clown White.

"Waaaaaay too short last time, Francis…"

"I'll be careful."

Chris the receptionist is just sitting there with his head lolling on his neck, a big mess of a noggin on top of a stump, all wrapped in a bubble of The Morning After. He wants to know what the deal is with Taffy's mom, wants to have a big ki-ki about the whole thing after work, wants to drag me along with him to Splash for happy hour. I never go. Once, I did. Once, I went with Chris to Splash.

We hadn't been in the bar for ten minutes before Chris was whooping it up with the early drinkers, everyone knowing everyone by name. Even in a big city, when the circles get smaller as people die and bars close, the ones that gather daily under the cover of sunlight keep a place for the next one at the bar, and names get remembered. Torches get passed. That's what happens. Glitter tossing isn't inherent to anyone; it is a learned trait, the nurture to nature.

"Eww, fish," Chris said.

The bartender laughed and did a little number where he ran back and forth behind the bar rubbing his arms and saying, "Unclean! Unclean!"

"What's that?" I said. "What's happening?"

"Why," said Chris to the bartender, "has this place suddenly turned into a tuna boat?"

"A tuna boat?" I repeated. Chris wasn't listening to me. He was busy bonding with the shirtless bartender.

"I mean, not for nothin' but, ah, there's only so much flannel one Queen can handle! Haaaaaw! Isn't there a different place for them?" Chris seemed drunk already. He always did.

"I wish," said the Cro-mag bartender, his disgusting nipple hairs brushing the stack of clean glasses. "We used to be just a men's bar."

"This is a men's bar," I said. "I mean, a queer bar, right? What are you guys talking about?"

"We're talking about the school of fish that just swam in," Chris said, making the fish-swimming motion towards three women who had walked in.

"Poor thing doesn't even know a fish when he sees one," said the bartender to Chris. "Are you sure he's one of us?

"Oh, yes, girl, he's one of us, believe you me." Chris said, patting my thigh, leaving his tapping hand there until I pulled it away. I was so confused.

"One of you? Whadda ya mean? A fish? Am I the fish?"

"Oooh, girl, you've got a LOT to learn about being a faggot," Chris said, trying to pat my thigh again.

The women passed behind us and took a seat in a booth. Two hot butches and a fence-sitter. I could tell she was a fence-sitter by the way she twirled her hair up in a bun. She was young, with those big doe eyes that can lay hearts out cold on the sidewalk. I could picture her with either one of the butches, or both.

The more stone of the butches put one big brown hand onto the knee of the new girl, forcing the blood to rush her white temples. She started rocking back and forth with every squeeze to her knee and I was, too. Rocking. Back and forth with the beauty of a new gay emerging, right in front of my eyes, ripping her cocoon to pieces and eating it.

It was like a nature documentary when you see a captive monkey set free to the wild, the moments of indifference and worry that lurk at the edges of the jungle erased once the monkey finds her tribe. I'm always excited to see people being actively recruited, the realization that the world is theirs for the taking lights up their faces until the day they say it out loud: I'm Queer, I think. *I think I'm queer.*

"We don't doooooo table service," said the bartender, "uh, *ladies.*"

Chris held his nose with his pinky in the air as the dyke walked up to order drinks for the table. He was waving his hand in front of his face, really playing it up, dirty-diaper style.

"Why are you guys so mean?" I said. It finally hit me that they were being cunty, parroting some hateful pip they were mentored by in some small-town gay bar, before they moved to SF and became assholes.

In that moment I was so glad to have been raised around women. My sister's friends never called each other *fish*, and I only remember the pejorative form being used in junior high. How I avoided these hateful queens for this long was beyond me. Maybe because I didn't go to the same bars. Glitter fear had paid off. It always does.

"Honey, I don't do no fish," said the bartender, "…and I hate when they come in here. They tip like shit, too. Probably because I don't have a pussy." He grabbed his tiny bulge and shook it at me.

"Looks to me like you have a pussy right here," I said, pointing to Chris, "a giant one."

"Oooh! Girl! You're learning fast! That was dishy! Serve it up steamin', girl! Work!" They both snapped their fingers. Chris and the bartender kept calling each other *girl*, yet they would only refer to women as fish. I was so lost in the jargon. All these years of being a cocksucker and I still couldn't tell if being called "girl" was a compliment or a total dis.

Girl. Girls are awesome, I thought.

"Why do you guys hate girls?"

"Ewww!" they both screamed at the same time, as if the question itself had been dipped in sardines.

"What?" I said. "Jesus H. Christ!"

"I don't hate anyone," said the bartender, lying. "I just think it was better before."

"Before what?"

"Before those fish came in here, drinking up all my beer," Chris said. "Get it now? Girl?"

Chris's derogatory obnoxiousness in calling women "fish" had never occurred to me inside the salon. At work I only take certain bits of information and blot out the rest. I never really heard it, not like this. In the absence of clients and blowdryers, Chris's words were now pure, blowing clean through the space between our barstools, and in this smoky light, I could see them flinging themselves at me. The bartender was just as bad, cartoon bubbles of hate arcing over the tap for Bud Lite, the "Bud Lite" logo shining in a rainbow font on the mirror behind him. Gay beer. Anheuser-Busch must really be down with the gays.

"Well, those ladies are gonna have to come up here to get a drink, 'cause mamma's tiiiiired," said the bartender, throwing on his ACT-UP! t-shirt. Sitting among the separatists I tried to imagine what it was like to be a girl in a bar — even a queer girl in a queer bar — wondering why so many gay men hate me, why they talk shit about me and push me out of their bars, charging me an exorbitant cover charge on a free night, telling me I'm not wearing Levi's and Leather so I can't drink there.

Looking at Chris's reddening face and his self-proclaimed diva-ness (yes, I have tried before to explain to Chris what diva means, pointing out that there may only be three living divas on the planet, that it's not like a new movement or anything, but still he calls himself a diva), I saw inside of his gin-soaked pores the entirety of his identity: *Gay*. He was gay. Chris is gay, everybody! Gay, gay, gay! And that's all he is. That's it. After *gay*, good luck finding other defining traits.

"I'm gonna go," I said. "You guys are gross."

"Hey! That's not a good dish, bitch! That's just shady," said the activist bartender.

On my way out the door I stopped at the booth. "You guys shouldn't give this bar any money. Fuck them," I said, pushing through the side exit. "They're assholes. And they don't even like you."

After I left, the stone butch got up and walked over to the bartender, right near Chris. So exciting. I was so riled, just waiting for her to throw a bottle or crack a good solid punch to his jaw. She lifted her left hand out of its place in her tight pocket. *She's a lefty, like me*, I thought, *fuck yes*.

With her right hand still in her pocket, she took her left one and lifted it to face-punch level, just a few feet from the bartender's nose. She curled up her lefty and released three long fingers, holding her pinky finger down with her thumb. I read her screaming lips through the window. "Three Bud Lites."

She probably even said "please" and smiled, her head bobbing to an acid-house re-mix of *We Are Family*. I walked home through the park and looked at all the weird heads making their ways to wherever it was they belonged, vowing never to go anywhere with Chris again. But still, he asks every shift.

I'm as guilty of poking fun at odd head shapes as any hairdresser. Jherri's melon head still cracks me up, but Jherri's not eleven. And Jherri knows she's got that big old water head, she's almost hyper aware of it.

Taffy only knows what her mother wants her to. Taffy's job is to sit with her headphones in and vid screen on and get worked on, and to not think of Big Wheels. Taffy has had more salon visits than Jherri has in thirty-six years, and now her face is being made quick work of by her surgeon-assisted mother. Had Taffy been born so waterheaded as Jherri she would have been killed on the spot. Shaken to death in the hospital room.

The first time I had Taffy in my chair she was nine, with Botox and Restalyne applied just around the eyes. And mouth. "Just around the eyes and mouth," the mother told me, "to make her look more awake. My little sleepyhead! Ahhh, she always looks so sleepy in pictures!" Her speech became staccato with frustration. "...So. Sleepy. In. Pictures!" she said, slapping the back of her left hand into her right with every beat. "Ahhh, Whadda ya gonna do... I mean, what can ya do?!"

Nothing. I can do nothing.

Taffy was less bruised up this visit, her eyes had un-swelled enough so she could see her new pig nose. It made me think of that episode of *The Twilight Zone*. She'd be fine there, in that dimension.

The mother never leaves Taffy's side, pulling up a chair next to my cutting stool and chatting about the young movie stars, she knew all their names, where they were from, and how much they made. She talked a lot about how much they made.

"Taffy, look!" Her mother was holding up a copy of *Teen World* magazine opened to a glossy pictorial of a small blonde girl wearing heels, a micro-mini and a gold T-shirt that said *Little Bitch* on it...

"Taffy, look at Teena Macteeny! She looks like a doll! An absolute doll, no?" Taffy could smell the picture being held inches in front of where her nose once sat.

"I don't like Teena Macteeny, Mom." It shocks me to hear her speak up for herself, that voice.

"Yes, you do!" her mother said to her, then turned to me. "She just loves Teena Macteeny."

Taffy packs her head with earphones, says, "I *don't.*"

"Oh, you don't even know what you like, Taffy," said her mother's back, her face to the mirror. She's spraying dry shampoo into her hair in sweeping arcs of mist, scrunching the product in and up with her hand, head tilted to one side, then flipped to the other.

She does this once or twice an hour, regardless of location. Bank lines, wedding receptions, the middle of a sentence — no place is safe from her recital. Spray, scrunch, flip, repeat. The bigger the audience, the more times she repeats.

During the shampoo show, she leaves her Balenciaga bag crooked on a chair, its wide mouth open for the audience to peek into. In a moment of voyeuristic intention, you can see three thousand dollars transformed and stacked as tiny jars of caviar face creams, scrubs made out of placenta, and thick emulsions extracted from nightingale shit and monkey blood for tap-tap-tapping under the eyes. "Nothing works like monkey blood!" she told me, pulling out the jar and showing me the label, the price-tag a blur of zeros. After the final scrunch I sat the mother down on a cutting stool, and sat Taffy in the chair to finish the consultation.

"So nothing too old, Francis."

"I gotcha. Something girly."

"Girly, but not too fifth-grade girly, you know? You know!" (I don't know. I never know.) "Taffy's turning into a little woman, right before our eyes!"

Taffy stiffened, terrified of what that meant. A little woman. So far, it pretty much sucked. Her mother seemed pretty happy, though, and had lots of money, so that was good, right? Lots of money was good.

But her new nose hurt. It looked like it hurt.

"So, should we do the Mohawk, Taffy?" I say.

Taffy smiles a small break, covering her invisible braces with her hand. Her mother's face constricts, which probably hurts. If I were her I'd avoid bad news altogether, or anything that pulls the face. Laughter, sadness, anger, all made more complex by the searing pain accompanying them. I can never tell if she's happy or sad. I'd bet on sad.

"Ohhh nooo, Francis… no Mohawks! After last time we were in she didn't stop talking about Mohawks for two weeks. Do you know what she told our maid? She told our maid that she was getting a Mohawk! I about died, right there on the bottom step!"

"So, no Mohawk, Taffy. And no shaving it. Let's just do a little clean-up. C'mon, let's get you washed." I say.

"Okay, Francis."

When I lay her head into the sink for washing I can see right up her new nose. This is not out of the ordinary. When washing old men's hair you can see right up into their sinuses, with all the coarse white nose hair coated in snot.

Standing above her and behind her head she looks like a puzzle that got cut up. The area of skin between where her top lip ends and the bottom of her nose begins has increased in size, where you could lay a quarter on it with room to spare. Her top lip is mangled ground veal, the whole of the mess always shining with spittle and lip gloss.

"It's still healing," explained the mother when she brought Taffy in the second time. "Her lip," she tapped. "Still healing," she said from behind her hand.

It doesn't seem to have healed up quite right. New skin. The old inner lip became the new outer lip. The juxtaposition of the new nose with the new top lip is out of control. I try to make normal talk with Taffy; I can't imagine how it is for her when she's away from her mother. Kids are so cruel.

"How's school, Taffy? If this water gets too hot you let me know, honey. Just scream or something and I'll cool it down… so, how's school?"

"It's okay. It's a lot of girls." She's rolling her cell phone around in her hands.

"No boys?"

"No, yeah. There are some boys. I like to hang out with the boys, and they jump off rocks and stuff but my mom doesn't like it."

"Why not? Why does your mom hate it?" I ask, changing her verbiage. *Why does your mom hate you?* is what I want to ask.

"She says I act like a boy," she says, and all of a sudden nothing could seem any simpler. It always takes me so long to check in.

"How's your nose?" I say, changing the subject from bad to horrible. Yet another reason I am not cut out for this work. I need to know too much, and I can't get all my information from the scalp.

"It's gone… it's gone and now I have this piece left…" She was bonking her feet together hard. "What if when I'm done I'm all pieces, Francis?"

"We're all just pieces, Taffy." *Ridiculous. We're all just pieces.* I didn't even know what that meant. "I mean, we all have things that happen… things that are awful… ya know… and we pull it together… again and again… all these pieces, ya know?" As I talk, I scrub her scalp, long raking motions and thumb pressure, release points, giving her a great shampoo. As always. If nothing else, I give one hell of a great shampoo.

Pulling up on her right temple, I felt a small amount of give, a detectable amount of pressure release from beneath my circulating fingers. When I looked down, I could see that I had soaked the skin around Taffy's nose, causing a swelling red circle to form around the base. The right nostril seemed off. Stretched. The skin that was healing was now taking on a whitish appearance, her right nostril flaring tight.

I pulled her head from the bowl and threw a towel on her head faster than I rinsed it out. Her hair was sopping under the towel, and where any normal person would have done more to make the child comfortable, I instead pulled away horrified. In front of the mirror I could see the swelling more pronounced. A large half-moon formed around the nostrils, cutting across the middle of her small face, she seemed like an infant. I back away from them, too.

"Get the mother in here, Chris!"

"Sh's comin', honey," Chris slurs. He's drunk. I can't stand when he drinks and does coke at work.

"Go home, Chris. Get the mother in here and go home."

"She' shoppin', honey," Faggot code meaning: You're gonna be stuck for at least another half-hour. Mother ain't picking up, none of that, so, yeah, she' shoppin'.

"Oh my God, what happened to her, Francis? What did you do to her?" came the voice before the face. The mother.

"She's fine!" I sing. "I'm cooling her skin down with some cucumber!" I make it all look innocent, as if every day a kid's nose begins to peel from its mooring, me trying to explain why my high pressure shampoo may have just blown tens of thousands of dollars in surgery costs. Trying to explain why I am sitting here pressing cucumber from Chris's take-out cold sesame noodles against the space where a little girl's nose used to be.

"Dr. Vaguen said this could happen, the red ring. It's going down now, right? Huh, Francis, do you see it's goin' down?" Spray, scrunch, flip.

"Uh, yeah, it's going down…," I say. The terror had begun to leave my chest, the visions fading. I was sure I'd be held responsible for ripping Taffy's nose from her head.

"They're kids," she says, as if there were thirty kids there and we were co-parenting. "They heal. Taffy's going in next week for a consultation." *Consultation.* I wonder how many times Taffy has to hear that word every week. Such a serious word, for any person.

"What is she going in for? I say. "Fix her nose?"

"Whadda ya mean, *fix her nose?*"

"I was just… I mean, just that her nose, and the water, and everything… It, well, I wasn't sure… I just…"

"Her ribs."

"Her ribs? What about her ribs?"

"We're removing them. The two bottoms."

"Two on each side?" I brace myself against the chair.

"No, just the two. The two bottoms! *Kkt, kkt!*" She says it like I'm being stupid, does this pointing routine, "one… on… each… side…, ya know? One… two! She needs that hourglass figure… She's a little tree-trunkey, don'tcha think? Dr. Vaguen thinks, ya know, with the ribs and some hips, it would give her some shape." She made the curvy-smurvy hand motion.

"Shape?"

"Yeah, ya know, shape! Lookit Teena Macteeny… You seen her lately? She looks fan-tastic."

I waited until the last moments of my session to tell Jherri that I quit, filling the hour with cosmetic chit-chat, me answering Jherri's questions about what to do now that her head stubble is growing in. She looks like an exotic fruit, fuzzy like a kiwi.

"Jherri, I can't do it anymore. No way. No fucking way."

"Do what, Francis?"

"My job. Cut hair. Touch people. I can't. Can't do it."

"Whadda ya gonna do, Francis? Just quit?"

"I already did."

"Shut up," she said. Jherri was getting too familiar with me. I wasn't her little brother, and even if I was…

"I won't shut up, Jherri. It's done. I already quit. Told 'em all to fuck off."

"Francis, if I may, your language is very telling. You're not a big swear-er, and now you come in here with the *fuck this* and the *fuck them's*… I dunno…"

"Don't know what, Jherri?"

"I dunno, I mean, you seem like… irrational. Knee-jerky. Do you think they'll give you your job back if you apologize?"

I jumped out of my seat. "My job back? I don't want my job back! And apologize for what? For the little girl with her nose taped to her face or for the old lady who feels like shit because she can't afford face cream? You tell me because I didn't do that, Jherri… I didn't do anything."

"Calm down, Francis." Jherri wished she had a button to push, beckoning Tammy. "So, okay… You quit. Nothing you can do now…"

"Yup." I was proud of myself. I hadn't told anyone off when I quit. I hadn't thrown my stuff around screaming. "I just quit. Told them it wasn't a match and walked out."

"Wasn't a match?"

"Yeah. That's what I said. Isn't that what you say? It's not a match… I thought that's what you were supposed to say when you quit, or if you were firing someone… *it's just not a match*."

"I guess so…" Jherri's never quit or been fired in her life. She's in a genuine state of worry for me, imagining herself in the same position. She shakes off the image of her hand accepting an unemployment check. "What're you gonna do, Francis?"

"I guess I have to look for another job." Every follicle buzzed my scalp when I said it out loud. I hate it, looking for a new job. And I hate getting a new job. That awful first week where you find out who hates you and who doesn't like you. You have to get there early and look like you care, in the sad pleats of your black Ross uniform. Mine are so worn that the fabric inside the pleats is darker than the rest of the pants. There were pleats involved. Who would hire me?

"Where will you look for a job?"

"I don't know, Jherri. The interweb… the yellow pages? Is that a thing, the Yellow Pages?"

"No. It *was* a thing, it was a thing called the phone book, remember?"

"I'm going to see if I can get a job at a school. I'm gonna call around."

"A school? Don't you need to be a teacher to work at a school? Or do you mean, like sweeping up or something. A janitor? You want to be a janitor, Francis?"

"No, a Beauty School, Jherri."

"But still, you need to be a teacher. This is a good long-term plan. I support this."

"I can be a teacher now! Why not?"

"You can't just *be* a teacher, Francis. Not in a school, anyway."

"Well, I'm not going to teach door to door, Jherri. And I can teach at a Beauty School. All you need is a license in California."

"A *teaching* license."

"No! A cosmetology license! Any hairdresser can do it."

"I think you may be wrong. Do some research and we'll meet next week."

"Not wrong. I already did the research. Believe me, if my school was any indication, anyone can teach at a beauty school. It's where old hairdressers go to die. It's what we do. That or sit on the State Board of Cosmetology."

Jherri was angry at my prospects; angry that I thought I had it all wrapped up and wasn't losing my mind about quitting my job. "Well, we'll talk about it next time…"

"You're brushing me off, Jherri, like you're right and I'm wrong."

"Now you know how the rest of the world feels, Francis… time's up."

"Well, I still do have one more client to see before I'm done. I'm going back to the salon for my last appointment. I gotta tell Miss May."

"I said time's up, Francis."

Her shield is white, with the capability to turn invisible. In place before the mirror, we waste no time. Miss May, this will be our final visit.

She has been so important to me I'm not sure I could prove she was real. My strongest psychic connection, my only ally in this horrid place. With all other clients, I had to resist psychic connection and empathy. Fight it, even. With May it was organic.

Before I can say a word, May and I fall into the crack in the mirror. The one on the right hand side. The caustic tang of hair dye is overtaken by the smells of a carnival midway: funnel cakes, roasted peanuts, candy apples, and motor oil. May never was one to ride the rides but the whirling lights of a Ferris wheel, spinning in perfect circles, always took her breath. I look at her beautiful face. Her eyes close for the blessing of her dream. I look away for a moment and then fall in. *Coney Island, 1963.*

Beyond the setting lotions and the reassuring blue-black of Barbicide, the infinite vortex of reflection produced by opposing mirrors becomes our backdrop; endless images of ourselves bounce from surface to surface until we are mere specks at the finest point of an eternal tunnel.

The ghost figures merge when we enter the mirror. In trance state we watch teenagers and young girls on blind dates riding the Parachutes and sneaking kisses behind the rubber ducky booth.

May and her Sailorboy sit on the west side of the boardwalk, at the first empty bench from the steps, just above the restrooms and far enough from the throngs of people waiting in line for red-hots at Nathan's.

Sapphires dance on the tips of waves as May rails into some nervous small talk about the Navy, what a S.E.A.L is and why he has to wear his uniform while off-duty. It's all so silly to her, this protocol. "Who would know whether you wore this monkey suit or your birthday suit?" May has no respect for anyone who isn't capable of breaking a rule.

"Fleet Week. We gotta wear the uniform all the time," said Sailorboy. "It guarantees respect and sets us apart from civilians." All this talk of rules and respect makes May hot and furious; her disdain for patriotism is enough to clear a room. Sailorboy cuts off her oncoming tirade with a clanking, toothy kiss. He was chewing green gum. She kept feeling it slide across her tongue and thought she'd die.

May hates gum. So do I. Especially mint green gum. Nobody looks stupider than when they're chomping on a piece of gum, smacking and talking and making that loud CRACK sound that makes me jump every time. If I want to chew, I'll order dinner.

After an eternity of kissing and dodging chewing gum, the first fumbling hand on May's breast forces an inhalation so sudden it threatens to suck up the ocean before her, to wash over her insides with salt water and stars. To smash my mirror to bits, its silvered glass imploding with the cans of hair spray and the picture of Rowe Mesa, the hairdryer, and the swirling lights of Coney Island.

Sailorboy is riding the Cyclone, alone in the front car. May won't get on that contraption. *I ain't buying no ticket to die*, she said. He cranes his neck at every turn of the vibrating wooden track, trying to spot May. She should be standing by the chain-link fence waiting for him, like the other girls standing by the roller coaster, scraping the bottoms of their penny loafers across the hot pavement in unison, little kicks to the gravel.

Sailorboy thinks he catches a glimpse of May as she kicks off her shoes and walks towards the boardwalk. She won't stand among the cosmetic yarring of the Penny Loafers. She flips her perfect hair and is gone. The track snaps his head around again and he pukes into his lap. May makes her way down Surf Avenue, towards the screaming chaos of the Bowery, and never does look back. Until now, really. A half-smile curls her mouth as our eyes meet in the mirror, the other stylists coming into focus as they flit about the salon.

"Sometimes I don't want to come back, Chach."

"Me neither, May," I say. "Me neither."

All of our visions now sealed in the mirror at the crack in the top right hand corner, May says, "Puppy love," waving her hands in front of her, wiping away cobwebs of memory.

"Maybe he's still alive," I say. "In Indonesia or Long Island somewhere. With your name tattooed on his arm in that Navy green ink."

She laughs and we think for a minute that he may be out there, thinking of her in a dream. Or not. I'm pretty sure he's dead. She seems convinced. I comb her hair and we both laugh but the mirror shows regret in her green eyes and the mirror never lies. Then she remembered the gum and regretful eyes turned to eyes that hate, as if she would've killed him now for the gum back then. She now remembers why she didn't turn back in the first place and she's glad she kept walking.

"He was an officious ass, that Sailor. *Fleet Week*. Give it a rest," she says. "How's it going up there, Cha-Cha?"

"Wonderfully splendiferous, Miss May." I say it like Daffy Duck, a return to the silly back and forth, making up words. Broad smiles cross her face when I fawn over her. If we could rip our hearts out and melt them together we'd be either a psychotic, pill-popping eccentric, or a hard living, devil-may-care neurotic. I guess that perhaps we've already done that. Melted together, I mean. In the mirror, the mist is getting cold on the boardwalk. Time to go. We get up off the bench, pigeons shooed away from feet. No more bread.

"Give us this day our daily bread, pigeons…" May laughs out loud. We take one last look at her dead sailor waiting on the bench for May to come back as the lights of the rides begin to flicker up to meet the Brooklyn sky. Her body jerks once and she is fully in the salon, smiling. Remembering, I think. Maybe not. Maybe she's just smiling because she's made of gold.

"Do you think my curls will kink in Belize?" she says.

"I'm hoping not, hon. I cut it so it holds its curl."

"You do! I'm sure it's just perfect, hon."

Why can't all clients be like May? Is she the only one? I love the way her flesh stretches across her bones, sinews shining. She has vitiligo, where the skin loses pigment in small patches over time. On some days, May will apply a small dab of cover-up but usually she lets her vitiligo flag wave proudly. The vanity of it all perplexes her.

"Listen to this, Cha-Cha: Plastic surgeons in Beverly Hills are removing ribs from fourteen-year-old girls in order to give them an hourglass figure. Reprehensible. I say kill the surgeons. The kids would be better off living in dumpsters with all their ribs, original chins intact. Don't you think, hon?"

"I couldn't agree more, May. Line up the parents and shoot 'em. They don't know beauty. Cutting everything up." All I can think is Taffy, all in pieces.

If it was up to the other stylists, Miss May would have all her grey blended out or tinted over. They'd swoop into her head and tell her silver hair is ugly, if she'd only let them. Before she'd know it, tiny rods would be wound tight around her lashes, followed by the application of ammonium thioglycolate (a caustic). After five minutes, the stylist would rinse, blot, and apply a neutralizing solution (typically sodium bromide or sodium perborate). May's closed eyes will leak flames while they kill her with cliché: "Don't worry, sweetie. Don't forget: you gotta suffer for beauty."

It's not true, you know.

That's why May doesn't go to the other stylists. Too pushy, she says. She tried them all until she found me. She ignores them now like strangers; she won't bear their interrogations on why she won't ever tint her hair. She's shocked to hear anyone but me speak to her.

"Hello, ma'am." May looks up to see a salon assistant, eager to please. "Can I get you some tea?" She's a nervous girl who started last week, going around offering drinks, sweeping up split ends, doing laundry, cleaning the toilet. *Assisting.* I like her. The skinny mean girls give her a terrible time, though, letting her believe that she'll be fired if she doesn't scrub the toilet and fetch them coffee.

May didn't hear the offering of tea, she was fixed on the girl's smile, locked into her strange eyes. The assistant, Detta, had eyes with beatific asymmetry, the left one wide open, the right one more narrow and sleepy. Her hair shot out in spirals, a halo of black and premature silver, two feet in diameter. "Would you like something to drink? Ma'am?"

"Hello, dear," May says, before waving me forward to stage-whisper in my ear. "Who on earth is that one?"

"New girl," I say.

"You look out for her, Cha-Cha. She seems sweet. And she's one of us, dear, just look at her. Gorgeous in her sparkly white bubble, I tell you what. Absolutely gorgeous."

"I know! Detta's gorgeous, May. I see all white with glitter. And you know how I hate glitter, May!" Detta's shield doesn't drop glitter about, thank God. She imagined it that way so that the glitter sticks only to her protective armor and doesn't jump off, a design which shows great compassion and forethought. I noticed it when she dropped off her resume, when she looked at me out of the corner of her all-knowing right eye.

"I hope she doesn't quit, May." I was hoping Detta would take May on after I left.

"Oh, she'll quit, Cha-Cha. They all quit."

She's right. This industry chews up people like Detta and me. I want to tell Detta to run, now, as fast as her glitter bubble can take her. I want to take her with me, wherever it is that I'm going. But I need to leave her here to care for May.

May sighs at her reflection, the last clouds of hairspray dissipating from around her chair. "I'm tired today, kiddo." She says it every time she's in. By the time we're done, we're both exhausted.

"It's okay that you're tired, May. I know what you mean. Believe me, I'm tired, too."

Detta cleaned my mirror while May and I collected our things and headed for the door, the squeak of the squeegee filling the street as we walked out.

"She's a very nice girl. Very driven." May was looking through the window, Detta squeaking away in her glittery bubble. "Poor thing, in this world. She has no idea yet."

May's eyes went soft as she took a deep breath, absorbing the smell of the street. "Ah, well, I'd love to chat all day but I have things to do, Francis. See ya next Tuesday, Cha-Cha. Don't be late." She clicked her cheek, *cck, cck*, and turned before I could tell her I was done. Then May turned and walked away, towards the church carnival down the block where the Ferris wheel was about to light up the ripped Mission sky.

III

V i•sion•ar•y (vɪzh•ə•něr• ĭ) *adj., n., pl. -aries* 1. given to or characterized by fanciful or unpractical ideas, views, or schemes: a visionary enthusiast. 2. given to or concerned with seeing visions. 3. belonging to or seen in a vision. 4. unreal or imaginary: visionary evils. 5. purely ideal or speculative; unpractical. 6. proper only to a vision. *--n.* 7. one who sees visions. 8. one given to unpractical ideas or schemes; an unpractical theorist or illusionist.

The ad read: *Visionaries Wanted at Hair Smile Academy: East Bay!*

Perfect. For some reason I thought, perfect, I'm a visionary by which I meant: *I've had visions.* But there's a difference between the Old Testament definition of visionary and the new Corporate Culture definition. One is seeing The Risen Christ like a painting burning behind your red shades and not being sure if it was a dream. The other is, according to the dictionary, a schemer.

When I called the number, the person on the other end answered with, "It's a beautiful day here at Hair Smile Academy Orinda. This is Derek, how can I help you make magic today?"

I froze. Long intros always leave me expectant. When I was sure he was done selling magic, I said, "Hi… I saw your ad on Craigslist looking for… well, the ad said… visionaries. I was wondering if you need teachers as well." I was only half kidding.

He laughed like it was the funniest thing he had heard in at least a week. "Our teachers are visionaries! And yes, we need 'em! Let me patch you through to our Educational Director, Maureen, she'll let you know all about it! Hmmmm… I'm just the front desk."

After such an unreserved phone welcome from just the front desk, I figured the Director of Education would be even more excited to talk to me, so glad to have a potential employee on the line that they would sing a round of "For He's A Jolly Good Fellow" before she started talking.

"Hi! This is Maureen! I'm the Director! Here at Hair Smile Academy! Derek told me you saw our ad! How can I help you make magic today?!" Again with the magic.

"I'm calling because I'm interested in the visionary position?"

"Awesome! Are you interested in making magic?"

I went silent. I wasn't sure that I had called the correct number anymore.

"Is this a school?"

"Mmmm, yeah, I mean yes, it is a school, but it's so much more than that! I mean it is a school, I don't mean to confuse you, but it's a very magical school offering a top-notch educational experience to our Learning Experts!"

"I'm sorry, come again?"

"Hahahahahaaaa! I'm so sorry; I often forget that people don't automatically know the lingo of our culture!"

"Uh…"

"SO, inside of our culture, we don't call them students, we call them Learning Experts. And our instructors are called Learning Coaches!"

"Wait, wait, wait. I thought they were called Visionaries…"

"Oh, I like you already! You are cracking me up! See, we are all Visionary Leaders, both Learning Experts and Learning Coaches alike — all Visionaries. I'm a visionary, too! Inside of our systems we have three different types of people. The people we aim to celebrate are our *visionaries*. You'll understand more when you take a tour and get a feel for life inside of our culture."

"Inside of your *culture*?" My head was spun. I hadn't heard anything else she'd said.

"Yes, inside of the culture of our schools, we consider it a breeding ground for learning. It's what sets us apart from other programs. The culture has to do with the systems we use, the language we speak, and the accountability we have for one another. Don't let it scare ya! We really are one big happy family here at Hair Smile Academy East Bay!" She was really getting into it. I just wanted to know if she had a job for me.

"I would love to give you the opportunity to visit us and see if you'd be interested in joining us! It's so nice talking with you!" I hadn't really said much of anything but she seemed to think it was going well so that was okay I guessed. As long as they pay me in money and not magic beans I would be willing to give it a shot. "Can you come in and check it out today!?"

"Today?" I began shaking.

"That would be awesome, right?!" she sounded like she was jumping up and down. "I mean, what could be more awesome than that?" Tons of things. Tons of things could be more awesome than that. Never having to work again, for one.

"Let me check my book." There was no book so I shuffled some papers on the table, old zines, and a Safeway circular. I was still in my pajamas and already stoned. I wanted a job but not this quick. Everything up until now — the ad, the phone greeting, Maureen's desperation — should have formed a pinwheel of red flags but I was blinded by the potential opportunity to get a paycheck. I always go with my gut but this time I told my gut to shut it. "Nothing in the book," I said. "I can be there in an hour."

"Do you know where we are?"

"Well, no. I thought you were in the East Bay but then the receptionist said Orinda, so I may be a bit confused, here…" Maybe a bit.

"East Bay, Orinda…. tow-may-to, tow-mah-to," she said, "but yes, we are in Orinda."

"Po-tay-to, pa-tah-toh," I said, trying to cover my panic. She began jumping up and down again at my bon mot.

"I cannot wait to meet you!" she said. Click.

Orinda was not what I considered the East Bay. I thought it was some sort of valley. To get to Orinda, first you go to the East Bay, and then you drive for forty minutes over a sweeping grade. So it is a valley.

During the three-hour interview process I noticed nothing amiss. I had my brain closed as it was decided as soon as I saw the Help Wanted ad: *If they offer me a job I will take it.* A robot looking for work in desperation mode, they could have conducted my interview at a landfill and I would have only seen frantic dollar signs pushing up through the slop. Instead, they conducted my interview at the school in one of the many tiny offices. They asked me some standard questions but didn't show me around the place. I couldn't tell if it went well or not. I thought, not. Not well.

From the initial phone call with Maureen I had expected this big ceremony of an interview, something where I'd have to explain why I am a good team member (I'm a really hard worker), what my biggest strengths are (I work really hard), and my biggest weaknesses (I'm a workaholic and can't leave any project undone). In a regular first interview setting these cliché answers would have worked against me but at Hair Smile Academy it would have been just what they were looking for.

In her office, Maureen explained to me that I would be working with three different types of people here at the school, in a 50/30/20 breakdown: Visionaries/Resisters/Fence-Sitters. I knew what the words meant but didn't understand the equation.

"Okay, so, fifty percent of people are *Visionaries*... like you! Visionaries are people we celebrate, we love them the most! Then, thirty percent are *Resisters*. They are only here to learn to do hair. Resisters are only here to get a license." She said it like it was filthy to want the license, like all resisters should die.

"Isn't that why they come here? To learn hair? To get the license?" That's why I went to school. Maureen's hair, a shade I call *L.D.S.Blonde*, shook at my assumption. I was blowing the interview.

"NO! They come here to be better people. We have all sorts of people with such rich stories, Francis, I can't even tell you...," she said, and I knew that she was going to tell me even though she just said she couldn't, getting on my nerves. "Some of these kids come from broken homes, have no real direction until they come here. They're so broken, some of them!" She looked like she could cry at any second, which I'd learn was a common look for her.

"Oh," I said. I was still trying to figure out what my job would be. "So would I be teaching hair at all, or is it all just soft skills?"

"No, lots of top-notch hair teaching. But along with it, coaching. That's why we don't call our teachers 'teachers.' We call them 'coaches' or 'Learning Coaches.' See, Francis, this has to be about building human beings, above and beyond hair. It's about pumping up people and pumping up sales, to make more so we have more to give. We like to give back. Even when people don't ask, we give, give, give. We are always helping."

"So…," I said, opening my notebook, a symbolic shield thrown up against her last demonic statements. I pulled my filter in and began again. "So, the visionaries, the resisters, and then the fence-sitters. What happens to them?" I figured I had already blown it so I might as well ask a ton of questions.

"They are the ones we are here to motivate! When we praise the Visionaries, it motivates the Fence-Sitters to join the Visionary Squad. It's funner over there on that side! Believe you me!" When she said "funner" she applied an affected British accent, really dressing up its misuse.

I think of the fence-sitter back at that horrendous bar, Splash! — that girl with the butches. I had been using that term *fence-sitter* for years. They may have been visionaries, in hindsight, those butches. Compared to Maureen, anyway. They seemed committed to encouraging the Fence-Sitter to teeter, knowing she was no Resister. But the fence-sitter had all the power. She was the secret Visionary, had them all wrapped around her little finger. Sitting on the fence should be the new coming out.

"What do you *do* to the Resisters, Maureen?" I imagined a basement of students chained to work stations, Val dollhead skins pasted to their faces, noxious perm solution creeping in from bubbling vents.

"Ignore!"

"What?"

"Ignore 'em! That's what we do! Celebrate the Visionaries, Ignore the Resisters."

"That's your policy?"

"That's our *culture*," she winked.

"Okay, then. I don't want to take up too much more of your time," I said, backing slowly away from her desk. It didn't look like she was very busy, ever, but I wasn't ready to turn my back to her.

"We'll be in touch, Francis! We have a few other candidates to interview…"

"Oh, okay. I'll just hope I hear from you then. Thanks a lot." I left, knowing what *we have a few more candidates to interview* means. I'm jobless and crazy, not stupid.

Now I'd have to tell Jherri the interview wasn't as good as I had hoped it would be. She'll give me an *I told ya so*, tapping her eyes against her glassed-in master's degree. She's gonna try to send me back, I thought, Jherri's gonna try to send me back to Hello Gorgeous!

But three days later the call came. I didn't want to pick up because I didn't recognize the number but when I went to mash "decline call" I slid the thing the wrong way and it picked up anyway. I gave a fumbling hello, jogging the phone from one hand to another.

"Is this Francis?"

"Yes. Who's this?" I barked. I should monitor the way I get after people for their inadequate phone manners but it's an etiquette flaw I find unforgiveable. "You called me," I say. Wasn't everybody taught this shit before being allowed to use the phone as a kid? Doesn't it go along with *don't point*? It starts with a "Hello, this is _____, may I please speak with _____? I got none of that when I picked up, just the *Is this Francis?* "Who is *this*?" I repeated.

"This is Maureen from The School! So I am calling to offer you a position with us and was wondering how soon you could start training." She was smile-talking. Jherri had told me once that you should always smile when you talk on the phone because the person on the other end can hear it. Jim at TopQual used to say that, too: *You can hear a smile.* Maureen was smiling. I really could hear it. I didn't remember much from my interview visit, and judging from what I did remember, I never expected a callback.

"Is it paid training?"

"Hahahaha! Yes! Just like I told you during the interview! Paid training! It's all in your packet! You still have your packet, right?"

"Yeah, oh yeah, I have it, that packet. The one you gave me." I had no idea what she was talking about, there had been so many info packets and contracts stuffed into a three-ring binder and handed to me at some point but I don't know what I did with it. It must be in the car or it had disappeared within an hour of my return from the interview. My dog ate my binder.

What if this was some corporate mind-fuck test, where she was really holding the binder the whole time she asked, seeing if I would lie about it? I did.

"Okay, so read that and sign everything and we'll fill out all of your employment paperwork when you get here tomorrow." Maureen had decided that I said I would start tomorrow, when I haven't even said yes yet.

"Tomorrow?" God, please let that binder be in the car.

"Yes! Aren't you excited?!"

"Yeah. Yes. Yes, I'm excited. What time?"

"What time is it ... let me check my phone ... oh my gosh it's four-thirty. Whoo! This day has just flown!"

"No, I know it's four-thirty, I mean, what time ..."

"Oh! Hahhahaahaahahaha. You mean *tomorrow* what time."

"Yes, tomorrow. What time?" She was bugging me now.

"Haaaaahahahaha! How about eight a.m.?" She's hysterical to herself. I don't understand how she could laugh at everything and then tell me eight a.m. What's so funny about that?

"So, if you want to, you can get here around seven-thirty and get oriented. I won't be here so you'll be meeting with Bree, my Director of Education."

"I thought that was you."

"You thought I was Bree?"

"No, I thought you were the Director of Education..."

"Haaaahaha! No! I'm the School Director. Bree is the Director of Education." Everything's a hoot to Maureen. It must be an Orinda thing.

"Oh, okay," I said, "So I'll just see you tomorrow then."

"Seven-thirty! Don't be late!"

"Oh, I won't be late. I'll see ya..." I knew I still had the option of jumping off the roof of my house instead.

"Great! Ooookey-dokey then! I look forward to seeing you tomorrow, Francis! We all can't wait for you to join our team!"

My ribs tightened around my chest and I almost collapsed, picking up the feeling sent from her to me over the wires that connect my kitchen to the outside world. I now knew for sure that an empath could, in fact, do a reading over the phone — it had just happened to me without even trying. A vague sense of impending doom shot to my frontal lobe, escaping, swirling the room, and compressing my ribs. No matter how happy I wanted to be about my new job prospect, the bones of my chest would not give up their warning. Utilizing my only known coping mechanism that didn't involve needles or rectangles, I pressed my cheek to the cold linoleum of my kitchen floor and counted my exhalations.

On my first day on the job it all became clear. This wasn't my grandmother's beauty school (they told me that) and I found myself trapped. The Industry of Beauty had wrangled me into its lair, and I found myself employed by one of its largest corporations: HAIR SMILE ACADEMY.

As a student, Beauty School was torturous for me, so much so that I spent almost most of my time there in the bathroom. Class time was absorbed by my famous cartoons in the sidebars and the gratuitous barbs I shot at my fellow students. The targets of my animosity feathered off from the students, seeking the heat of the administration offices, and, most ruefully, the instructors in their lounge. It was a natural progression.

My former instructors at Marco Botelo School of Cosmetology and Hair Design were easy to mark. Such characters, I couldn't hold myself back from writing about them. Black humor shot from my fingertips with ease, leading me to convince myself that the rants were worth something outside of cheap-shot humor. Fueled by my own self-loathing, I transferred my hatred onto the shoulder-pads of my teachers. Now, decades later, I sit smock-ridden and surrounded by beaming young faces. I have come full circle. I have become an instructor.

When I got to Hair Smile Academy I was covered in sweat, having pedaled two miles on my bicycle from the closest train stop. A forty-year-old on a small-framed BMX bike. For clothing I was, at best, grasping at straws. An oversized white shirt that made me look like a failed poet. Black pants with worn and faded areas at the knees, indicating so much more than I ever wanted to reveal. There's always something they expect in this business and, never knowing what that looks like, I end up looking like a clown without makeup, yet again. I felt a million eyes watching me as I chained the bike's silver cross-bar to a news box, fumbling with the lock. So many eyes. Not a new feeling. I thought it was my Most Holy Guardian Angel blessing my day. *Thank you. Guide me. Don't leave me now.*

When I heaved open the glass doors, I saw the origin of the million eyes. Turns out it wasn't my Most Holy Guardian Angel; it was a double conga-line of students clad in flowing white robes, the same smocks from Marco Botelo's. The students lined up across from each other with elbows locked, their human chains forming a precise gauntlet for me to pass through, a tunneled version of a reception line. There was no way around. It was like the Spanking Machine from grade school.

As I stepped into their formation, which stretched a good thirty-five feet from beginning to end, they began hooting and hollering, just that way, too, using hoots and hollers. And claps. Lots of clapping. They high-fived me as I passed each of them, saying, "Welcome."

Welcome. Welcome. Welcome. Every single hand that I slapped was attached to a white person with white teeth and a white face. Lily fucking white, I was the most ethnic-looking person in the building, with my giant nose.

"Thank you," I said, curling up the left side of my mouth. I must have said it sixty times. *Thank you.* "Welcome!" *Thank you.* "Welcome!" *Thank you.* I wished they could have all said it at once. I wished I didn't have to pass through this line. I wished I had jumped off my roof when I had the chance, and I wondered if any of the Heaven's Gate people had wished that as well, that day as they ordered their last meal together.

As I passed they closed off the tunnel behind me, joining together as a mass of white. This part, I liked. I felt like Christ being followed by that mass of hippies during the "Hosanna" in *Jesus Christ Superstar*, and hoped that when I turned around they would all be waving palm fronds, enraptured by my arrival in their village. They would lift me high onto their shoulders, knowing by my smile that I was here to fight for them. To battle the High Priests of the Council on their behalf, the new Messiah, come to remove their shackles and loosen the restraints of boring lesson plans and forced smiling (Signpost# 2: Always Be Smiling. Fake It If Necessary).

When I turned around to wave to them, the sand blowing through my long Nazarene hair, they had dissipated and were already making their way to their lockers. They do this to every new employee and had been ordered to greet me like a king. Judging by the myriad wall posters all bearing the same bearded male face, it was clear that they were in no need of a new Messiah. They already had one.

Looking around this warehouse of beauty, I saw that a new cast of characters had replaced those who inhabited my old rants. Where once sat the misguided but genuine Miss Laura-Lee or the *Puppies In A Basket*-loving Miss Dot now sat the corporate, new millennium version of the beauty school I remembered. It didn't even look like a school. It looked like a high-end salon in Los Angeles.

There were lights everywhere, bright ones, with a forty-foot ceiling and exposed metal beams. It was a warehouse of beauty. A catwalk stretched along the long wall of the space, hovering above the clinic floor, for me to watch the action from. At first I was excited about the catwalk. I pictured myself standing there invisible, below me students buzzing around, busy eating cupcakes, sweeping up hair, consoling customers who were crying because their hair turned green.

Thick plasma teevees lined the building's short wall above the doors to the Scrub Shanty where the shampooing was done. The eight giant screens showed the same video in a loop, all day every day. The same images. There was no channel to switch, it was the only show there was, and I didn't know the source of the images. They were just there, repeating on the screen. By the end of my stay I could recite that video by memory, like Rocky Horror. *Here's the part where the girl smirks and flips her hair... here's the part where the guy takes off his glasses and turns... here's a crowd shot, with a man crying for joy in the second row, third from the left...*

My pipe dream of teaching at a Beauty School was devastated. The backdrop of my experience was gone, filled now with a super-cool team of the Happy to Be Here crowd. Hot Topic does Sassoon, with sharp lines all around, tattoos, piercings, nail polish and black lipstick, all working in opposition to the beatific smiles plastered on the faces of my co-workers. My team. Anytime I hear "team," I think "coach."

The chain of command inside of the school went from Maureen directly to Bree, or from the School Director to the Director of Education respectively. Bree was 23-years-old and had never worked in a salon. Zero experience in the day-to-day of dealing with a client, zero real life experience. And I bet nobody ever took a shit in her cutting chair.

Bree was groomed for this position from her first day at the main campus in Orange County. They saw it in her through the mopey strings of her mousey brown hair, saw that they could carve her into a True Leader of Visionaries. From her plain face they created what stood before me now on my first day. I was twice her age and she had an office. Instead of crying, I picked at my smock as she took her puffy seat.

Bree wore black on black, with shoes I would have picked up and then decided against in the late '80s. Thick monster soles, all black, with a black upper boot that shined vinyl, with grommets and colorful laces. "You gotta have color somewhere!" she said, which made me wonder if she could see her own head in the SUCCESS poster that hung on the wall behind me.

Oversized braids of neon pink synthetic hair sprung from her head in shrunken coils, a look created by melting the attached nylon hair with a fabric steamer until it's just so. It's a technique I learned in NYC in the '80s. I knew it well. The make-up she wore was more of the same, stuff I had seen at Pat Field's when I was young.

I used to have a similar look, if only more disheveled: shaved brows that can be penciled in if needed, pointy eye make-up, lip-liner up to there. The more I studied her look the more it made me think of the '80s and '90s, of the life I've lived, of the looks I thought looked good despite the evidence now seated before me. My past is her future, I thought. She's doomed.

"So… how are you?" She said it like she was talking to an ex-junkie with a strong relapse history. How she knew this, I'd never learn. She grabbed both my hands across when she said the elongated "how arrrrrre you?"

Signpost #3: Establish contact in two or more places. This was a rule I'd come to learn over my stay. When meeting someone, make sure to not only grab their hand but also place another hand on their shoulder or upper back; it comforts them while placing you in a control position.

"I'm fine, thanks! How are you?" I was pulling at my left hand, trying to yank it free. I wanted to begin my employment paperwork but she wouldn't break eye contact. Signpost #4: Maintain eye contact to generate trust.

"I'm grrrreat... I'm soooo excited to have you here!" She was talking like we were about to ride a roller coaster.

"Me, too! I mean, me too am excited, I mean, I'm excited to be here as well," I said. So stupid.

Bree laughed at me like I *was* stupid. "Are ya nerrrrrrrrrr-vous?" She bit her lower lip, scraping a tooth against the viscosity of its gloss.

"A little bit," I told her. "Mostly about the dress code. Frankly, I'm not used to having one so I'm not sure exactly what I need to get for tomorrow."

"You've never had a dress code?" She was justly shocked. There are few corners of this industry where a person doesn't have to adhere to a dress code.

Bree's mirrored contact lenses looked me up and down, I could see my pathetic shoes in her irises as she assessed my costume, their image lingering when she raised her eyes back up. I tried to maintain eye contact but all I could see were my uncomfortable feet on display next to her pupils.

"Okay, so, the dress code..." As I started writing it down, she snatched the Black Warrior #2 pencil out of my hand. "Use this," she said, handing me a glitter pen with a feather on the top. "That'll be yours!" She clapped. "Yay!" She threw my pencil in the trashcan behind her, my left hand following it all the way until I heard its eraser clink at the bottom of the can. My favorite.

My hand adjusted to the girth of the new glitter pen, a nightmare of a writing tool, its feather tweaking my nostrils as I hunched. Please God, let it be black ink. I wrote DRESS CODE at the top of the page, my hand smearing the goo discharging from the pen. It was gold ink with gold glitter, the same as the shaft of the pen. Unreadable.

"Do you have a different pen?"

"A different pen!" she said, holding out a bucket of day-glo ink sticks.

"Oh, I uh…"

"All my pens are gliiiiitterrrr! And I picked the gold one just for you! It's yours! Your pen!"

I felt so ungrateful, looking at my sad face in her bubbling eyes. "Okay," I said. "Okay."

"And the gold looks sassssyyyy, huh? Like youuuu, Furrrr-an-siss! Sssssaassyyyyy! That's why I picked it, daaar-lin!" She did this clumsy ballet with all of her words, stretching them to their limits at the beginning or end. She would drop her voice a full octave between syllables or go up at the end. She couldn't just say something. I would learn that she does this with all queers, trying to slip into the lingo, as it were. The Orange County version of a fag hag, she would vote against anything having to do with me breathing but still feels the need to tell me that glitter pens, and glitter in general, is *fieeee-erce*.

"Glitter is fieeeeee-erce, huuuuun-ey," she said, her black lipstick like a Grinch. "Now you write wit' dat' pen, guuurl." She assumed the diction of a hag at a Harlem Drag Ball, making me embarrassed for the entirety of the human race. The central air clicked on, re-filling the room.

"Okay, so dress code?" I was trying to convey grudging respect over quiet resistance, something shallow bitchy. I couldn't unleash on her. Not on my first day. I kept my eyes on the paper. "Dressss cooooode…?"

"Everything on top is fine," she said.

"On top?" I didn't realize she was speaking about me right at that moment.

"Yeah. Your shirt is fine."

"Oh. Okay." Shirt fine, I wrote, the words fading in gold.

"But you need to have some flair. Don't be afraid to be *you*. I have a feeling you are fieeeerce, Francis, and we want to make sure that all that fiercenessss doesn't get lost here. The dress code isn't about killing your creativity, by any means. I mean, look at me!"

I couldn't. I wasn't sure if she meant it literally or not but I sure as hell wasn't looking up at her, with those creepy I'll-be-your-mirror eyeballs that echoed my own desperation. How could I be doing this? How could someone care so much?

"So, Francis, you pretty much have three choices for your total look here. First option would be classic. I don't really see you in a classic uniform…" I knew what she meant. Classic must be the black on black, or black or white, shiny shoes look. The way Mark James dressed his assistants. *Classic.*

The next option after classic was *dramatic.* I imagined this look to be more of the same, black on black, only with a little extra sass, like a banded collar with fake eyeglasses. Skechers.

"I'm not very dramatic," I said to Bree. It was true.

"So, then the only option left is exactly where I would have placed you… *fashion-forward!* That's what I am," she said. "I'm a fashion forward, too… so, you're gonna need black pants. And those shoes… uh…"

"I can't wear these shoes?"

"Neeeeewp! Soooorrryyyyyy! Not those!" She laughed. She laughed at my shoes. I thought they were fine. They were the only shoes I had that weren't canvas. They were fancy Canadian dress shoes, for chrissakes. I bought them when I was 19 at Allston Beat in Cambridge, but never really wore them. Who cares if they were older than Bree? They fit. I hadn't considered that besides fitting properly there may be some other criteria for footwear, and I was insulted by her giggles. Look at your own fuckin' shoes, I thought.

"These are fancy," I said. "My shoes…"

"They look too sneaker-y. And if you can run in 'em, you can't wear 'em to work." Another rule. If you can make it out of a fire without breaking both ankles, you have the wrong shoes on. "And soon we are going to Vegas for Conjunction! Yer gonna need to look feeeeee-ierce, hun!"

"Conjunction?"

"Oh, you'll see. Conjunction is where the magic happens. It's so exciting you've never been! You get to meet our Head Coach!" She grazed her fingernails across the pewter frame of a photograph as she said the word "coach."

"Him?" I asked.

"Yep. Tedd Godman. He's so... I can't explain, I get all goosebumpy! He's our head Visionary, and boy, will he get you goin' on this stuff."

Now I was nervous. Nrrrrrrrrrr-vous, even.

Conjunction — not *The* Conjunction, but only the one word, *Conjunction* — was open to everyone in the Hair Smiles Corporate Family and nobody else. If you went to a school and you sold enough bottles, you were therefore family, and were to attend Conjunction. If you worked in a Corporate Salon and were burned out, maybe you needed a little mental boost, a refresher course on the Corporate Culture, Conjunction promised a little healing to send you back into the game.

Conjunction is always held somewhere glitzy like Vegas or fun like Epcot. It doesn't matter. All these people need are a Civic Center and a giant screen. Walking in, brushing past velvety curtains and displays, the thumping gay bar techno overrides even simple conversation. Runways, smoke machines, curtains that are lifted. The whole audience smiling like they were on fire with the spirit of the company. And they were on fire, absolutely; I could tell by their eyes, eyes with the same amount of dilation as the cripples getting healed by evangelists.

Swelling music, dancers behind white screens, doing G-rated wiggles in shadow boxes, and fifty-foot screens with projections of the products, all while hair models balance ridiculous hairdos on their heads. The cutting and styling done at Conjunction is done by the corporate higher-ups, the faces you see on commercials and ad copy. People drool watching master haircutters like Swatanovski slice simple curves into a model's hairline before sending her clodhopping down the runway to a sea of waving arms. There's a lot of arm waving, like at a concert in the '80s during a power ballad. Slow and rhythmic, all the way left, all the way right. All of this for hair models. All together now.

Platform Artists perform, one after another, sashaying around their models to the same techno music that is played at the school, only here it has a louder and more persistent thump with a higher high end plus sirens. "Baby, you're a firework!" they're all singing, dancing, their motions limited by the folding chairs lining the hall. They're ecstatic in their dance, at least on the inside; the more adventurous ones move into the aisle and really let loose, showing they were not Resisters. I was worried I'd be spotted.

The music started doing a strobey rock and roll thing, *loud quiet loud quiet* like a band from the '90s. This seems to get people back into rows, organically filing from the aisles and fanning themselves with programs. And then it goes silent as the lights dim to almost burn-out. The opening theme of *Close Encounters* begins to go, *bah bah bah buuuuum.*

The crowd holds their breath until Steve Long, the Academy Founder, makes his way out onto the stage. "The Man Inside the Magic," reads an enormous banner unfurling behind him, his face printed above the words in an eight-by-ten foot tribute to himself. People scream like he's The Beatles. All four of 'em.

He holds his arms humbly at perfect right angles, palms up. His beard is impeccable, traversing his giant face with geometric accuracy. He waves to the assembly, then does an *Oh, You!* with his hands, moving his palms down to say *Enough, guys! I'm human, just like you. And by making this motion, I show you a humility that you could never hope to understand.*

People take the edge of their seats, looking at him. *Look at him up there, Brian. It's really him. Right there.* Steve does a full three-sixty revealing the keratinized manifestation of his ego: his long, skinny ponytail. It drips over the back of his black blazer, a perfect assemblage of hair and product, tight elastic at the occipital bone. *Look at his ponytail, Brian. It's, like, perfect.*

Other men in the audience have scrunchies in their hair in homage but in comparison they all feel weakened by their attempt. Not enough Shine Drops.

Steve Long does a short set, keeping his talking points to charity work and fundraising. Him being the owner, I had expected more. He listed four or five charities that he gives to, that *we* give to, he said, and the room went blank. He paused for it to sink in. "I say *we*, because *we* are a team. You are all on the bus. And I thank you from the bottom of my heart."

The crowd is silent as they absorb the intensity of the way Steve Long said the word "we." We. All of us. You and I. You and I and Others. Calm settled over the room and for the first time, other than the sniffles arising from the I'm-Trying-Not-To-Cry dudes, you could have heard a pin drop.

Being "on the bus" was a big part of the culture. When asked who was on the bus, you were to respond with "I AM ON THE BUS!" That big, too. Huge letters. When asked whose bus it is, the stock reply is "YOUR BUS, STEVE LONG. IT IS YOUR BUS, AND WE'RE JUST ON IT."

After a few beats, Steve Long surveyed his misty-eyed minions, who were mostly white and hetero, before exiting stage left with a final "Namaste" (deep bow, rigid prayer hands). Ninety percent of the crowd thought that "Namaste" was like "Aloha" or "Ciao," words they often used but didn't know. Brand new words. If history has taught us anything, it is that hairdressers love the New Things. Just like the New Colors, the New Words were, well, new, and even if they didn't know the spelling, they used them.

I had noticed this at the school back in Orinda. On Saturday before breaking for the weekend, Izzy would write "Have a grrrreat weekend! Chow!" on the Celebrate Victory dry-erase board. *Ciao* as c-h-o-w. Maybe it was intentional and she meant for us to eat a lot over the weekend. I shouldn't judge. I'm picking Izzy apart. But she begs for it.

Other New Words flew around inside the culture of the school, exotic new words carried in on the backs of slick ponytails. *Karma* is notorious in its wrong context usage. Someone on daytime teevee has promoted the concept that "Karma is a bitch," and now its copious use has defined it in those terms.

"Don't forget, Karma's a bitch," Izzy told me when I asked her to cover the end-half of one of my shifts. Not even a whole shift, either, like two hours. I didn't have a doctor's appointment or anything; I just wanted to go home. I do this at every job, not only jobs at cults. The morning allows me to somehow muster the strength to face the day, the train, and the possibility of marshmallows but somewhere along the course of the day it all shifts.

By noon I am convinced that I am not the kind of person that is able to work for others. If I were sold into white slavery, I would be a real lemon. By two in the afternoon my thoughts have turned into an evil genius, hell-bent on getting me out of there. Some backwards manifestation of self-preservation kicks in and the only thing that matters is escape and the cozy jangle of an early afternoon train, free of commuters. Just me and a few other people who couldn't handle the world for two more hours share a car. Hands are folded and magazines are opened and then closed, eyelids too heavy to read. We relax until our respective stops. Whenever I do this I feel guilt upon getting home to my couch. Before I can count to ten, the two hours that I left early for have already passed and I'm in the same position I would have been later only without the pay. Still, it's worth it, every time. If you are ever wondering if you should leave work early the answer is always *yes*.

Leaving early or calling in sick is easier than explaining to a room full of people, mostly Mormon teenagers, the theory behind Karma and how the incorrect over-usage of the word in my classroom is driving me bonkers. "I know Dennis took my banana clip, that horrible little faggot," LoVerne will say, "but he'll see. That Karma'll get his ass." Her friend, Keith, will holler across the room "Karma is a motherfucking BITCH, Dennis! Watch your ass, motherfucker!"

It exhausts me to monitor these interactions. In the span of two sentences some students can say a multitude of offensive things, blowing my mind. Do I start with You Can't Call Dennis A Faggot and

Why, or do I begin another lecture on Karma, on how it's not a bitch by nature but more of a cause and effect type of thing. A leads to B. Planted seeds will grow with care, I'll tell them, asking if anyone is familiar with St. Paul's letter to the Galatians about reaping what you sow. But then I'd have to explain the difference between sowing and sewing. Can of worms. So I give up. I admit to being over my head. Keith doesn't care what Karma is. Not yet and maybe never. In the eyes of my students I am an old man.

When I see myself from outside my bubble I still feel nine years old. Isn't that what they say about drug addicts? That the brain freezes at the mentality of when you did your first drug? Am I a nine-year-old in a 41-year-old body? I think I am, thinking back to being nine, before I ingested drugs other than coffee and teevee. I didn't even start smoking cigarettes until twelve. Acid at fourteen, and pot all the time. So maybe I'm not nine. Those first three joints at the party, and the acid and grain alcohol when I was fourteen would indicate that, emotionally, I am at least fourteen. Thus would be the result if my case file was presented to a professional addiction specialist: "You are frozen at fourteen."

I wonder if my teaching style reflects this frozeness, if I am still terrified of the mean girl's lunch table and the jocks. Then Keith says to Shawna, "Girl, what are those stupid skippies you have on? Where'd you go, Payless? You feel good?" and I remember. Horrible Keith. I hated him like I hated the jocks and the mean girls' table, and I want them smashed now as much as I did in seventh grade. If I am frozen at fourteen I am frozen at my first FUCK YOU, leaving no desire to suck up to my students.

After Steve Long left the stage, while the "ay" of "Namaste" was still ringing through the collective ear, the room began to flicker with anticipation. At any moment, I thought, they would begin howling for an encore, but this crowd was waiting for the next speaker to step up. It turns out that the "Man-Inside-The-Magic Show with Steve Long" was only an opening act. He was the comedian that comes on before Ellen starts taping or the guy that warms up the audience for Oprah.

His game was getting the crowd loose for the big reveal. Steve Long was the morning energizer for the ultimate Pow-Wow, and my extremities drained of blood as the seconds ticked away the arrival of the Main Event. The guy next to me was crushing a travel-pack of Kleenex, the sheets useless, already soaked with sweat.

A loudspeaker voice began the introduction, a howling on the level of YOU WANTED THE BEST AND YOU GOT THE BEST, THE HOTTEST BAND IN THE WORLD, KISS! only there was no promise of flames, no blinking letters, leather heels, or clown white. Instead, the voice said: Ladies and Gentlemen, It Is My Pleasure To Introduce, The Man Behind Your School, Your Dean of Students, Your Beloved Head Coach and Leader, Tedd Godman. The voice said his name like this: *Teeeddd GOD-mannnnn!* The voice used more than one exclamation point.

The spotlight couldn't have been brighter or more on point in the way it bathed him with white during every step. From wings to podium he floated on a pillow of dry ice. Cameras flashed a lightning storm around him, his teeth a disco ball.

When Tedd got to center stage he looked at the podium, examining it from bottom to top, like a visiting alien looking at a DeSoto. He knocked on its wood with two knuckles, deadpanning the crowd with a "what the heck is this thing?" look. His act was to illuminate how cool he was. He was so un-stuffy that he couldn't even recognize a podium when he saw one.

"I'm gonna need to move around, heh, heh," were his first words to the crowd, who went apeshit at the thought of him moving around. Like they forgot he could. A peon came out and removed the podium, Tedd giving him the "get this thing outta here" look the whole time, smirking asides to his audience. Once the squeal of the podium being dragged back into the wings ended, he screamed "Helllll-LOOOOOOOO VISIONARIES!"

The people that hadn't turned to mush in their seats jumped to their feet, waving their arms — all the way left, all the way right. "YOU!" he screamed to a woman in the balcony, then he began pointing, "and

YOU, and YOU and YOU! You are ALL Visionaries! If you weren't" — *wurnt* — "well then, if you weren't" — *whirr-ent* — "well, you wouldn't be here this morning, now wouldya?"

Tedd sized up his crowd for a good minute, keeping them waiting, before he began his spiel. The image of people sitting starched in their chairs fed his mania and he wiped his bald head with a white rag. If he threw that rag into the crowd it would be as revered as the Shroud of Turin, but he put it back into the pocket of his black blazer. Maybe later.

He makes quick movements — arms up, arms down, thumbs-ups. One of his trademark moves is the full round-about, where his hand high-fives several points in front of the crowd and then forms a compete circle with his arm, brought down to slap the air in front of it, right about the knee. The spotlight person really had it down, following Tedd's quick turns and toe-bouncing with a can of focused wattage. Those things are heavy, and the operator was somehow able to capture every wink and shuffle. Somewhere in the building there was a professional.

Tedd goes into his speech on why we are all there. To energize. To re-fuel. To make Magic. All of his talking points spin and bleed into one another on the screen behind him, PowerPoint in full effect. People sway with his words, mumbling prayers and Baptist Church-worthy whoops of approval.

"A guy came up to me, says, 'Tedd, how can I be a better person? How can I be a Visionary, a Leader of People?' …and you know what I say to him? I say, Lose some weight. I say, Get your hair done. Stop being late. Stop being such a mess all the time. Then you become a Visionary, a Leader…" He smiles when he says this, keeping us all in on the joke. If we were there, he couldn't possibly be talking about us, right? He must be talking about some other losers, from some other school. At the Academy, we were all Visionaries. Resisters can go to hell.

On the screen behind him came the PowerPoint text, all accompanied by pictures of happy faces with new hair. It said:

Leaders Show Up! Leaders FOLLOW THE SYSTEM! LEADERS CREATE MAGIC! Then it went on: Leaders give others something to smile about. Leaders share their gifts and talents. Leaders Serve, Solve, and SELL! The word SELL blinked on and off, sliding across the screen, corner to corner, the font flipping into infinity, disappearing and then re-forming S-E-L-L, S-E-L-L SELL SELL SELL!

"See?" said Tedd. "See?"

I didn't; I didn't get it. He wanted us to sell shit. That's what I got. All around me the other students were basking in the light, all high vibrating, I was left flat. They all started hugging at the mention of sales and I wondered if it was mass hypnosis.

"And if you wanna sell, well, if you really wanna SELL, then you gotta look the part! Be the Visionary that you are! And you, and you, you, you! Nobody wants to buy shampoo from a fat shlump! If you wanna be cool, you gotta look cool. And that's that. And I love you. For all your work, for all your fundraising, for all you give and continue to give. Don't stop. Stay on the bus. Get others on the bus. Because whose bus is it?"

Some people screamed, "Your bus!" while some yelled, "Our bus!" which gave Tedd quite a giggle. It seemed like some people even just yelled, "Bus!"

"Noooo!" he said, then got serious, like *learn it.* "No, it's Steve Long's bus! It's the Hair Smiles bus! Ya jokers!" With that, he gave us an extended "Thank you, I love you." He held his palms together and bowed and the crowd went to sniffle-quiet. He was satisfied. He left the stage, and the house lights came up, the wooden podium already being dragged back to its spot.

By the end of Conjunction Weekend, all of the family is recharged with a joy for jargon and ready to take that joy back to their individual schools to spread it like a virus. Conjunction was the yearly Pow-Wow that kept the wheels turning back home, and those wheels would be kept in motion by several daily Pow-Wows at the Academy. Now that I had been immersed, I couldn't imagine my next move. All I hoped was that my Resisters seat in Hell was next to somebody good, and as far away from Tedd Godman as possible.

Back at the school, every morning would have its own Pow-Wow, which required all Learning Coaches to arrive fifteen minutes early. Pow-Wow was billed as a time for catching up, for energizing and stretching before beginning a day of Magic-making (Signpost #1: Always Make Magic), but behind its veil lay the real purpose of Pow-Wow: sales.

Called "bottle goals," numbers were set as to how many bottles of shampoo, conditioner, and hairspray were sold the previous business day. These bottle goals dictated how well we were doing as a staff. We rarely discussed the student body, curriculum changes, or individual issues. All of these were overshadowed by the engine of sales forever roaring in the background. Now that we were back from Conjunction, money was back at the forefront.

"Sooo, did we make our bottle goals yesterday?" Maureen would ask with crossed fingers, wearing a face that scrunched up in anticipation of a big fat NO. *I really hate this part, you guys, but I have to ask.* The answer was almost always "No, we didn't make goal." Her rainbow pencil tap-tap-tapped on the clipboard she balanced on her thigh.

Her leg shook up and down, that thing where if you balance just right on the ball of your foot it sends your leg into some simian response of rapid vibration. Maureen would do that during any meeting, increasing the tempo of the pencil on the clipboard to the point where you want to rip it out of her hand and break it, forcing her knee down to stop the twitching chaos that is Maureen.

The appointed Pow-Wow leader of the day would be the one to tell Maureen if we made bottle goals. On days when goals were met, the staff would applaud, a few of them jumping clean out of their chairs in a shocking squeal like my mother's friend, Alma Lancaster, used to do during a particularly invigorating exorcism.

On most days, when bottle goals were not met, a pall would fall over the room, until the words of Dr. Norman Vincent Peale would slide from the dry-erase board and massage us out of our negative thought patterns, ushering in a new framework of positive thinking, endless possibility, and increased shampoo sales. After bottle goals were processed and put aside, Maureen would remind us that Pow-Wow was about fun. Put an exclamation point after it. Capitalize it.

The staff, all seven of us, would sit around breathing, the Fun Coordinator of the day giving us our energizer, an exercise to shake out the nerves and accept the perfection of the day ahead. We would rotate duties every day so that the energizers were always fresh. Today was Devin's turn.

"Devin always does the BEST energizers," Izzy said. "Just waaaaiiit, it's gonna be awesome!" Accompanying "awesome" was a spastic double thumbs-up, her hands so excited they drained of color, her thumbs arching back towards her wrists in fleshy semi-circles. It looked like it hurt. Are you double-jointed? I wanted to ask but didn't. I had so many questions for Izzy but I knew to keep my mouth shut rather than open that door. I just watched her throbbing white thumbs — the exact opposite of The Fonz and Leather Tuscadero, the antithesis of 'Aaaaaaaaaaay!' — I watched them thumbs and waited for morning energizer to begin.

Devin walked into the office carrying a plastic punch bowl stacked with large Stay Puft marshmallows. There must have been three bags' worth of the big ones in there. Placing the bowl in the center of the table, she gave us all an open-mouthed smile and began the instructions.

"Okay, you guys know our morning cheer, right?" she asked, as if we could forget.

The morning cheer was done daily, at the end of every Pow-Wow. We'd all place our hands in a circle, full jazz hands beginning the chant: "Goooooooooooooooooooooooooo EAST BAY!"

By the time we'd reach the last "o" in "Go," the jazz hands would possess themselves with spirit fingers, the whole frenetic mess rising up over our heads after we'd scream "EAST BAY!" If we didn't scream it, Maureen would make us repeat it — the whole thing. With that face on, she'd say, "That one was kiiind of a bummer, guys! Come ON! Goooo East Bay? Let's do it again, please, guys? It sets the tone for my whole day! If we don't do it right, everything falls to pieces!" As if everything hadn't already.

Maureen's office was a study in denial. Clean as a whistle when you poke your head in the door but take one step behind that desk and witness an ineptitude that would explain Maureen's bouncing leg. Files stacked themselves from the floor to the knee; she can hardly roll her chair in. But somehow, morning Pow-Wow is to blame, the lame cheer is to blame. "Come on guys. Let's do it again, okay?"

So we do it again, this time with feeling. Form a circle. "Hands in! No dead hands, either. Jazz it up! Now, ready. Ready? Enthusiasm, guys! One, Two, Threeee…"

"Goooooooooooooo East Bay!" screams the group. Some screamed from being pumped up by Maureen's story, others screamed out of rage for having to do the cheer again, rolling their eyes as they yelled. I screamed because it was my job.

Devin's morning energizer began with the bowl of marshmallows being passed around the circle; with each pass we had to put one in our mouths and then say the cheer. With each round of bowl-passing, we had to add one more marshmallow to the swelling mass in our mouths and say: "Gooooo East Bay!" No problem on the first two passes but by round three my teeth packed themselves full, white sugar cementing their holes.

"GrrrrrrrrSttttByyyy," I said as best I could. My mercury fillings were throbbing, my mouth trying to pre-digest what it hoped wouldn't make it to my crying stomach. I tapped out after three rounds.

Izzy kept going, her underbite helping her hold in all the high-fructose corn syrup. Izzy had no leaks. Four, five, six. It was down to her and Jerrod, both of them drooling wads of white chunk spittle, wiping their chins with the provided rainbow napkins. Izzy laughed and the mass of jet-puff flew out onto the metal table, a meaty pile of chewed stretch landing with a wet slap. It was coming out of her nose and she kept laughing, snorting in and out, frosting pushing out the corners of her mouth and smearing her black lipstick.

A small plastic trashcan with the corporate logo was passed around like a spittoon behind the bowl of sugar, its Tupper bottom sucking the white chaw into its pores. Jerrod — the straight guy Learning Coach with the Boogens — beat Izzy and won the contest, his chin covered in a film of throat filth. There was no prize other than bragging rights. He did ten. *What a winner.* He was fired a week later.

Had I seen myself sitting in this circle, a dead person floating above a surgeon's table, with my teeth electric and throbbing down to their exposed roots I would have burst into tears. Instead I stayed inside my body, my eyes glued to the bottom of the spittoon.

No matter how strong an individual, when money combines in windowless rooms with a group of fanatics, it is easier than you may imagine finding yourself skipping breakfast in order to pack your gumline with an enamel-hungry sugar paste. It just happens, and in my three months at the cult I did a lot of things that I would look back on and ask myself *how*. How could you?

I should have never told them that I do cartwheels. It was an innocent lack of judgment on my part, in trying to join a conversation with my co-workers, something led me to say, "I love doing cartwheels!" In the months following I would have zero notice before someone would enter my classroom and shout through a microphone, "Doooooo a cartwheel!" and all of the other people would start chanting "Cart. Wheel. Cart. Wheel. Cart. Wheel," until I would put down my dry-erase glitter markers and flip myself upside down. All it took was one person with seniority to give the order and I would have to carry it out. I would turn myself over. I would do doubles. One-handers. Even the side aerials of my youth were attempted to add to the merriment of my students, who would go wild.

The students' reaction to my first cartwheel fed my clown veins with such a fury that I forgot where I was. I was on fire. Oh my god, they're laughing. Cartwheel. I wonder if this counts as my energizer. Cartwheel. Then I said, out loud, "I can juggle, too!"

Just as I realized the idiocy of the revelation and the inevitable outcome of saying, "I can juggle," there were three beanbags in my hands and a room full of shiny faces and Izzy, all going, "Jug-gull, jug-gull, jug-gull."

Where were these magical balls when I was a child with lotion and powder on my face? I used rocks my whole life, and now I find out that beanbags will appear in your hands when people say, "Jug-gull."

Through the haze of the whirling bags I promised myself to never say anything about rolling out the barrel, tightrope-walking, or balloon twisting for fear that by lunch I would be teetering on a rope spanning the distance between the school and the parking garage.

Every day after energizer we would group-hug on command, then break the huddle and run off to set up our classrooms for the day.

"Make sure there are plenty of stickers in the baskets, Francis. We're doing "W.O.W.'s!" Izzy said, like the boss of me.

I think W.O.W. stood for "Winner of the Week" but I can't be sure. W.O.W.ing was done every day before theory. The entire school would sit in my classroom and, in lieu of learning, they were instructed to give one another props for good deeds, exemplary work, or even special friendships. All kudos were accompanied by the application (from giver to receiver) of a smiley-face sticker to the smock. This phase of W.O.W.ing was called FACE-ing. F.A.C.E. —

Find what's good

Acknowledge the victory

Celebrate your victory

Enjoy!

It seemed to me that *celebrating* a victory and *enjoying* it may be the same thing but I kept my mouth shut. Izzy's thumbs. I just want my paycheck.

Keeping the acronyms in order was one of the more difficult assignments for me. Employees are tested on the acronyms and directed to incorporate them into their lesson plans. So when you have your 90-day review — if you want a raise — you better know what A.L.A stands for (Ask, Listen, Answer). There were constant learning and memory games in place to help you remember everything, particularly the name game, done with every new roll of students.

When Izzy did her cheer, clap, stomp, "My Name is Izzy, and I like Iguanas. I'm going to… hmmm… Iran, and I'm bringing, hmmm, let me think… an Indian! I'm bringing an Indian so the Iguana has a friend. *Ho-wah-wah-wah ho-wah-wah-wah…*"

I was horrified. "So the only reason you're bringing an Indian is to watch your Iguana?"

"Yeah, I hate Iguanas. And I don't want the Indian to get lonely."

FACE-ing was held at 8:30 sharp. Attendance was mandatory; lateness was out of the question. If you couldn't make it for the FACE-ing you weren't even allowed in the building, losing valuable clock hours, time a student would have to buy back later in order to graduate.

"Nope, it's 8:31!" Izzy would say to the latecomers, guarding the door like a Hot Topic chihuahua. Women and men in their forties would rush in breathless and terrified, knowing they have no choice but to submit and attend this Learning Expert circle-jerk every day. It was like junior high in the morning, where you have to go to home-room before any classes. A check-in. A FACE-ing. An ego stroke. Absolutely required.

After Learning Coach Pow-Wow, Learning Expert Pow-Wow and endless FACE-ing, I could begin my class. From the stage, I would strap on my Janet Jackson Rhythm Nation headset and scope out the lesson plan. All lesson plans must follow a formula, like everything else. I couldn't just teach. I had to do it a certain way. The layout of the blank lesson plan was an A) B) C) format, breaking the lesson into three pieces.

Part A was Introduction of the New Idea. If I was teaching skin care I could hold up a picture of a pus-filled pimple and say, "Does anyone know what THIS is?" Visuals were crucial to the process. The class would scream like they were being hacked up at the sight of the zit poster. During part A of the lesson I would incorporate P.E.P, or pep, to keep it all clear:

Point At The Object: *"Look at that machine over there…"*

Example: *"It's called a heat lamp, it uses infrared rays and Tesla currents to reach deep into the pores during a facial, I used one the other day on my sister, and her skin was glowing afterwards…"*

Point Again: *"That… is a heat lamp."*

Part B of the lesson plan would be the actual teaching part where I would explain what causes a pimple, the different kinds of pustules and when, if ever, to touch them with bare jazz hands. These are the questions that would be on the test. I would tell them, "This is gonna be on The Test," just so I knew the Resisters and Fence-sitters would listen and pass. The Visionaries hated that I did this, feeling cheated. The Visionaries were a bunch of Sweet Peas, and they bugged me. I'd always be a Resister.

Part C of the lesson plan was a re-visit to part A. The poster, again held up, was dissected by the students, now armed with a half-hour's worth of pus knowledge. The Visionary students becoming drunk with pus power during my verbal re-cap pop quiz: "Furuncle!" they would shout out. "Boil!" "Cyst!" "Melanoma!"

The Orinda school's franchise owner was a small Mormon woman wrapped in a giant black bubble. Sparkle black with no flexibility to its surface. Like Wet n Wild nail polish, it would crack before it gave.

I didn't see the bubble as I rounded the corner but when I slammed into the sparkly casing around her skin my body tensed up like a thigh muscle wrapping itself around a long needle. As my back foot pushed forward, her face was suddenly inches from mine, a fright mask of expensive make-up with bronzers filling the needle holes left by Botox, coral lip shine perfecting itself inside the edging of her liner. Her brows were hardly there, an orange/beige line distinguishing beginning from end.

By sheer reaction I screamed, still two inches from her face. Not an "Ooh, girl, you startled me" yelp but a full-on shriek like someone threw a rat at my head. My feet lifted, left foot first, off the ground away from her and I stabilized myself with the wall's corner. The sudden back-step motion caused an inadvertent eruption from my chest, tight. I tried to make it seem like I meant to do this whole slapstick so I quickly went into a sort of "shall we dance?" move, that thing people do when trying to get around each other in the aisles of crowded supermarkets.

She didn't startle back or notice the way my body folded with my hands entwined backwards, my legs crossed and my hip arching away from her like a half-moon pose in yoga as performed by someone who had just been pulled from the twisted metal of a car wreck. She didn't even register my scream to her face. The Universal Face.

The same face that all the ladies were getting, the Universal Face has two different versions: East Coast and West Coast, or New York vs. Los Angeles. New York has the angular, choppy face, where the nose is a harsh cut and the cheekbones are raised high and sharp, a face of all pointy bones perfect to slice the throat of a baby calf. Los Angeles has the softer Universal Face: puffy lip implants and soft rounded lines all around. On both coasts, the faces keep becoming more generic.

Decades later, for all the Page Six jabs she took during the '90s, it turns out Jocelyn Wildenstein was not a freak but a prophet. A vision of things to come. Soon, both Joan and Melissa Rivers would succumb to Jocelyn's vision, too lazy to design their own faces, getting sliced and chopped and tucked until they, too, looked like a lynx. Who's laughing now?

The Face remained motionless and sturdy, all teeth, and said, "Hi, you must be Francis," the words flying out of a trap door in the bubble and socking me in the jaw. I wanted to scream again but was still swallowing the embarrassment of my first outburst.

"I'm Terry… I own the school."

"Oh, hi, I'm Francis. You must be Terry." *Stupid.*

"Yes. I own the school… Are you headed for your classroom?"

"Yep! Time for theory!" My voice was high and shaking.

Pushing my cart of materials around her bubble, I attempted escape but she was hot on my heels. When I walked into my classroom it was quiet as a chapel. All the Learning Experts had fake notebooks out, looking busy in front of the school owner, *looking busy* being one of the most important lessons they had learned so far at this school. And I couldn't even take the credit. They taught themselves, serving me up some serious proud momma.

Terry took her seat at the back of the room where she could see everything. Maureen had informed the students, but left me in the dark on her visit. I can't believe the shits didn't tell me.

Had I known Terry was gonna be there I would have planned something gripping for the day's lesson, some fun chemistry experiment or a slide show of the zit posters, but I had nothing. My lesson plan was painted as a Q and A, more of a rap session than an A, B, C formatted lesson plan.

Maybe I could talk about customer service, how products are sold, and what the students thought of sales in general. This would be a good foot to jump off from in front of Terry, showing her that I wanted to push the agenda of sales, everything hinging on bottle goals. I strapped on my Rhythm Nation headset and began my loose lesson plan. As soon as I opened my book, Terry stopped me, yelling from her seat, "Aren't you gonna use PowerPoint?"

"Not today! It's Friday, that's our quiet Question and Answer day, and once a month we have movie day!" I thought she would be excited by my occasional loosening of the reins.

"Oh," she said, making a note in the pad she had on her lap. "So, we're watching a movie?"

"Well, we were just about to decide, the whole team, one Learning Expert, One Vote..." My students were used to this from me, this free-form lesson plan, but they knew I was in for it.

"What movie do you have?" Terry was pressing her crossed legs into the floor to contain her distaste.

The answer wouldn't pass my lips. In my bag I had three movies: *Flashdance*, *Female Trouble*, and *Shampoo*. None of these would cut it with Terry, I was sure. Whatever demon had possessed me to toss *Female Trouble* into my bag that morning was now laughing at my futility. "I brought a few movies..."

"Which ones? There are so many good movies about personal growth and success. Have you shown them *Ice Castles*? I love that one..."

"Seen it," hummed all the Students. Little liars.

"Ok... hmmmm, how about *Forrest Gump*?" said Terry. "That's always a good one..."

"No, I think we're gonna change it up. No movie day, guys!" The Learning Experts were upset but understanding. They were terrified of the Face, too. "Instead, I was thinking we could all do something nice for Terry!" Genius plan.

"Oooh!" she cooed, wriggling. "Something nice, like what?"

"Well, we heard you had a birthday coming up…"

"Aaaaand?" she was waving her hands down low like a marionette.

"Aaaand we wanted to make you some birthday cards!"

I knew this would go over fine. The students at the school spend hours gluing pieces of construction paper to other pieces of construction paper, all to the cheers of the administration. At their order, even. On Izzy's birthday they took three hours of furious gluing to get her fifty shiny cards that said *You're The Best!!!!* and *Thank You For Being You!!!* on them. Terry loved this shit.

"Jasmine, grab the construction paper! Ellie, get the glue sticks! And Jonathan…" I paused. Then, going against everything I hold dear, so awful that I had to brace myself against the sweeping tide of self-loathing, I said, "Jonathan… you grab the glitter."

Late again, I ran to the back of the building drenched in sweat, half-dead from riding my bike from the train to the school. I was always late on Monday. I wasn't sure if Terry was still visiting or if she had flown back to Salt Lake. I slunk around corners in case her bubble was there to slam me. On the table in the lounge was a note:

It was so nice to see you all! Thanks for doing a great job! And for the birthday cards! I love them! Keep up the awesome work!

xo Terry

Whew. She was gone. One bullet dodged. But it still seemed empty.

There was nobody in the Pow-Wow room, no music from the screens, not a co-worker in sight. At the end of the hall there was a sign taped to the door: Learning Coaches ONLY!!!!! I wanted to run. Things were being hatched in the Learning Coach Office, big things, this I knew and I couldn't go in.

Since I was already late and there was no Pow-Wow, I figured I'd take another ten minutes to smoke a cigarette, escaping the whispering coming from behind the door. I wanted no part of it, whatever it is. Like Groucho Marx, I'm against it.

After my break the door was still closed so I used the spare time to assemble the materials I needed for teaching theory: baskets filled with glitter pens, glue sticks, and bite-size Hershey's. My tools gathered and ready, I began pushing the dolly of joy towards the swinging double-doors of my classroom/theater. The gap between the doors was dark. On a normal Monday, this crack where the doors met would blast light from inside, the bustling morning voices of my students greeting me on the backs of the fluorescent green rays.

On this particular Monday, however, there was nothing coming from behind the doors. I began to think that my frequent lateness had caused me to miss some crucial information given during Pow-Wow, and that maybe I came in for no reason at all. Fuming over the possibility I could still be sleeping, I pointed my feet away from the doors until I heard a whimper slip out.

A drone of muffled voices and stifled sniffles became audible from inside the classroom and as I pushed through to the inner sanctum I realized that there was school today. The room was crammed with every student, teacher, and admin in the system of the culture of the school, from top to bottom — or bottom to top — depending how you look at it.

Leaving my rolly cart in the hallway I found my way to the back wall of the room and leaned against it, sizing it all up. The room was lit by a hundred sad tea lights, their tiny flames fighting the expanse of darkness that pushed at their metal-cup bases from the beams of the forty-foot ceiling. There were ten to fifteen fat scented candles, all white vanilla and spice wax, placed around the perimeter of the stage at the front of the room, their cheap smell burning pressure into the backs of my eyes. Pushing. Bree walked slowly up the steps to the top of the stage, dramatic as she grazed the candle flames with her bare hand as she passed.

Izzy was standing by the mothership controls, her itchy fingers on the volume button, ready to make the music swell behind Bree as she hit key notes in her speech. The scented candle headband tightened around my skull as I scanned the room for clues. Why is Bree walking up on stage dressed like she's going to a funeral? Why are there boxes of Kleenex on the table where my baskets belonged? All I could think was one of my students was killed by a drunk driver last night.

I began the tip-toe over to Izzy's post for an explanation but when she saw me coming she put a finger to her lips with her free hand, while her other hand made quick work of the skylight. She mashed the button marked SKYLIGHT OPEN/CLOSE, and the metal doors in the ceiling began to slide closed with a whirr.

I moved closer to Izzy but this time when she saw me she did the double-hand-slide, like the motion the home plate umpire makes to indicate safe; that motion. She ex-ed me out with her signaling as the skylight creaked the last bit of natural light out of the room and the candles obliged their pitiful takeover.

Aside from the tea lights and the migraine candles, I noticed two more candles on the edge of the stage, burning away, a foot from Bree's platform creepers in oxblood. The ridiculous shoes distracted me from noticing the shape of the candles that sat before them. The two candles on the stage were shaped like buildings. Two of them. Two towers. Two burning towers. In her hand Bree held an old yellowed newspaper and, cueing Izzy, she began.

A soft spotlight faded in just enough to light up Bree's pink extensions and allow her to read the front page of the newspaper she held, unfolding it as deliberately as a performance artist dropping a Twinkie into a jar of period blood. She held the preserved paper up like a piece of evidence, pinching its corners and panning it left to right for the audience to see:

"AMERICA UNDER ATTACK!" read the headline. Oh God, no. Please, no.

I checked the date on the calendar and sure as shit it was September 11th, a day I've blocked out with great success since that day in 2001. Now, eight years later, Bree stood on the stage and began reading, while the tower candles began to melt and bend into one another. *This*

morning the United States was attacked by Al Qaeda operatives at two
points; both the Pentagon and The World Trade Center were hit… as of yet
it is unclear as to wha….

I jumped up from my crumpled position on the floor, running for
the double doors. Bree stopped for a moment as I scrabbled across rows
of Learning Experts towards the red EXIT sign. Tears washed down my
cheeks and Izzy scowled at me for making a scene. She pushed me out
the door into the empty reception area, where I collapsed.

Devin came running after me to see what was going on, why I was
having such a reaction and why I wasn't sitting in there listening and
doing my job.

"What's wrong, honey?"

"This is wrong, Devin… this whole thing. Is. Wrong. What the
fuck is going on, Devin? What the fuck, the fuck, what the fuck is going
on…?"

"Shhhh," she said, rubbing my back, her touch turning my tears to
sobbing. "It's okay, Francis… it's okay to have feelings."

Izzy stamped out of the room, grinding her underbite. "What's
up?" She gave her head a quick side-to-side flip.

"It's okay, Izzy," said Devin, one hand up, fingers pressed together.
"I'll stay with Francis. He'll be okay. He's just having a SEE."

"Ohhhh," Izzy said, decrypting the anagram for what was happening.
It was an *S.E.E.* I was having a Significant Emotional Experience, that's
what I was having.

"But he's supposed to be monitoring the Learning Experts. We
need him in there. If he can make it." Izzy was insinuating that my S.E.E
was mere theatrics, painting me as a petulant drama queen.

"I can't go back in there, Izzy. I *won't*." I was a petulant drama queen.
And once *can't* changed to *won't*, it was a new ballgame. My S.E.E.
was now read as Resistance, and Izzy was pushing me to re-enter the
memorial service.

"We do this every year! I don't get it! What's wrong? I mean, why
won't you go in there? I bought all those candles. It's pretty!"

"It's not pretty. It's hideous and it's ugly… it's totally awful and I won't go back in. You can't make me." I sounded like I was eleven.

Devin waved Izzy away, telling her that I didn't have to do anything that made me so upset, telling her twice until Izzy slithered away with a bottom-jawed sneer. Devin resumed the rubbing of my back and the tears and snot began to flow again, even harder, harder than I cried on this day eight years ago. In that moment I decided that I loved Devin, and she felt it. We both did.

"I love you, Devin."

"I love you too, Francis... I love you, too..."

"I'm sorry to do this to you... it's so embarrassing."

"No, no, no," she said, now patting me like a sick dog. "It's okay to have a S.E.E. here, honey. This is a safe place."

"It's not a safe place, Devin. Not for me, anyways... I can't do this anymore. This is too goddamn much.... Nobody thought to tell me? Nobody thought to warn me that they were planning a funeral service in my classroom today? What the fuck?" I couldn't stop cussing, breaking a huge chunk in my in-school persona. For that moment I was not Learning Coach, but only Francis.

"Can I ask you something?" Had this been a normal situation I would have answered with "You just did," but I was too far gone. I couldn't even muster up sarcasm. This is how I know real mourning. This is how I register true pain, by monitoring my ability to make a joke and move on. A circle of snaps wasn't possible, no sardonic response flying off my tongue; I had been stripped raw.

"Yes, Devin?"

"Is this something you've never processed before? 9/11?"

"I guess not, huh?"

"Yeah, no. I think maybe it touched a nerve. Don't let the terrorists win, Francis."

I could picture Bree, still on the stage, cloaking herself in the gloom of jumping bodies.

"What? The terrorists? What's that got to do with me? It's not okay to have a funeral without telling people, Devin."

"It's not a funeral! It's a celebration of life!" She's trying to talk over the sobs of white people coming from the classroom. I can't take anymore, again, as usual.

"It's a Mormon Cult," I said. "This place has nothing to do with hair. And Izzy? That loser, Jerrod, or whatever his name was? Come on, Devin. There's no culture in your culture. It's all Cult. You guys really keep the cult in culture, I'll tell you what." I was starting to get heated and I knew there was no escape other than the door. It was over. "Devin, look, this isn't like the school I went to… this is like a mall. Mall Culture. It's a different kind of terror."

"That was a long time ago, Francis, the school you went to. We are so different from that! We have so much more to give than just teaching *hair*!" Devin was starting to sound like a lunatic like the rest of them. I regret telling her I loved her so flippantly, but I guess anything can come out during a Significant Emotional Experience.

"Yes, but nobody's learning hair, Devin. And I'm too tired to do any more cartwheels."

"I know, honey, I know," Devin said. "So… now what are you gonna do?"

On September 12th I called an emergency meeting with Jherri, not an easy task without an appointment. To enter the building I'd need to get through Tammy, sitting up straight behind her new bullet-proof glass encasement. She was busy engaging her core, remaining aware of how her lower back muscles constrict or release as her knees rest on the pads of her posture rocker.

"Tammy, I need to see Jherri… now…" I tried to whizz by her but she wasn't having it. Everybody needs to see Jherri now, making Tammy wonder if they know the meaning of *now*. The eternal pragmatist, she's riled by anyone who insults her with improper semantics. When people say they need to see Jherri "like, yesterday," Tammy feels a burning in her throat and bites down on her cheek, tired of explaining that booking an appointment in the past would involve time travel. It's like doing something "one hundred and ten percent," you just can't do that, it's not an option. When talking with Tammy, Jherri has to be sure to keep it at one hundred percent or below.

"Tammy, I know you're busy, I just…"

Still maintaining perfect posture, Tammy flicked her pen towards the waiting room to show me how many bodies were there waiting and how I'm not special in any way. When I heard Jherri's voice, I broke. This was it. I would see her with or without permission from Tammy. The way I had it, I'd never be seeing either one of them again after today, another burned bridge sucked into the relationship chasm. I tell myself: this is last hole I will ever need to leave behind. I step over its carnage, and see that all's quiet down there where the burned bridges lay. No bodies, no flames. I pushed through the turnstile with its one-way *click-clack*, the counter logging every turn of its ratcheted arm. I was the 89th visitor of the day. Now inside, I could corner Jherri in her office.

Tammy peeled her bellybutton away from her spine for a second and deflated, then remembered who she was and jumped to her feet a little too fast for the posture contraption that held her upright.

"Francis, NO!" she said, mid-pratfall. Her calves wedged between the wood kneelers, she fell face forward into the glass of her cage, her cheek skidding down its surface and leaving a greasy slide mark. The weight of her fall dragged her down, her hands clutching at the meek wires of her keyboard and white noise machine, pulling all of it on top of her in a pile on the floor. I wanted to start clapping, it was so well done. She, too, was way past Dick Van Dyke. I had no idea. I wondered how she could hold in laughter as she crawled over to the turnstile, dragging the seat behind her in a figure-four leg lock.

"Francis… NO… No, Francis…" She was throwing her arms at me from the floor, one finger wagging, acting like she was standing up instead of laid out on a thin beige carpet with a pile of Ikea boards chewing at her legs.

My laughter grew too big to hold in, the throats in the waiting room all joining in, and even Jherri had to run to her office and close the door. Nobody asks, "Are you alright, Tammy?" as she begins to untangle herself. She remained composed throughout all of this, this prize-worthy fall and crawl, and she still seemed to be trying to work her abs.

I slid into Jherri's office, where she is still in a fit of laughter over Tammy.

"Oh… hi, Francis," she says, wiping real happy tears away. "What are you doing here on a Tuesday?"

"Jherri, I can't do it anymore," I say. "I'm leaving the city."

"Well, you can't just leave, Francis. I mean, let's be real. Get your head out of the clouds. Ah, did you see Tammy's spill out there? Good one, ah?"

"Why not? Why can't I leave? It's not like I have anything waiting for me here. Nothing is about to break for me in San Francisco, Jherri…"

"Escape sure sounds nice on paper, huh, Francis?"

"I don't see the Cons list, Jherri. I really don't."

"Yeah, well, you call me in three months, tell me how your big plans work out. We can talk about the Cons then."

This is what all therapists say when you give them incredible news. A big huffy *Good Luck With THAT* comes out when you think you're telling the best news ever — "My landlord changed my lease to month-to-month." "Good luck with *that*…" "I'm gonna try lucid dreaming." Pfffft. Ha, yah, good luck with that. I'll see ya on the other side! — It never works with therapists. They always shit on my dreams. Jherri will not be the exception. For the first time, I see her heart pounding and I'm smiling.

"I'm moving away."

"You can't move away. Away from what, Francis?"

"Just away."

"You can't run!" She says this at every chance she gets which, in her field, is pretty often. She hates to see people go; people get so trapped by social work jobs.

"I'm not. I'm not running away, Jherri. Maybe I'm running *towards*, ever think of that?"

"Running *towards*? That's not even a thing, Francis, running towards. You're just running away. Oh, yes, you are! And what're you planning to run toward, anyways?"

Ugh. Jherri is loving this, thinks she's on the brink of figuring me out. Her hands are rubbing clammy together, and she begins tearing up scrap paper. Now *she's* on fire.

"I don't know, but not hair. Not more scalps." I can smell Jherri's scalp from here. "Not more scalps... Who knows? I can juggle... that's all." I'm pulled in so tight I can hardly see anymore.

Jherri's smiling wide, all those teeth again, annihilating her stack of scrap paper. I don't even know why I came to see her. *riiiiip.* "You know, Francis..." *riiiip,* "Nobody wants a clown, not a forty-year-old clown, or not a clown at all. People *hate* clowns, Francis, and it's stupid, anyways... And you know why you can't go? Because *No Matter Where You Go, There You Are!*"

"Jherri, come on now."

"It's TRUE, Francis! It's totally true. The poster is totally right."

"I'm not living in a poster, and neither are you. Pull it together, Jherri. And it's getting gross out there, getting worse."

"So you run!" She seals it all with a note in my chart, looking at me like I'm bleeding out right in front of her. She's drooling. *riiiiip,* "You can try to go" ...*riiiip...* "Try to run..." *riiiip,* "but you'll only be stuck with yourself."

I'll only be stuck with myself. That's her best advice, that I'll be stuck with myself.

"There are worse people I could be stuck with, Jherri. And, anyways, I already have my ticket."

Possibility began swirling around the room, sparking the instinct to fight that I once carried around, this ancient response that I hadn't felt since fourth grade came spitting to life in an atrophied synapse. My teeth began to grind and I was wanting to get into it with Jherri. Everybody needed to fuck off, and Jherri's head, now blurring into a bubble of orange, was my best target. But I couldn't shoot. Even Jherri, with her head like the side of a barn, I knew I couldn't hit from three paces. I'm out of practice.

"I gotta go..." I said.

"Well, haaaaa..." She was shaking like a toothy monkey now, wringing the shredded scrap paper in her hands, hopping up and down in her seat. "…Good friggin luck! ahaaaaaa! Hey… Tammy! Francis is leavin', says he's gonna be a clown!"

Tammy was lying on the floor, letting the hardness soothe her back. Jherri couldn't see her back there. Tammy kept her mouth shut.

"Didja hear that, Tam? A clown!"

"See ya, Jherri."

"Yeah. See ya… probably see ya' next week, even! A clown. Francis, really!" She was laughing like crazy by the time I got out the door.

"Bye, Tammy," I said to the feet poking out under her desk.

"See ya, Francis, good luck," Tammy said, pushing into an upward dog. "And, hey Francis, don't listen to Jherri. I mean, *really*…"

When I got to my transfer point in Texas I decided to sit for a while and figure out the grand plan. Let the direction come to me. Push Jherri's voice out of my head. I let the inside of the bus station wash all over me, all gray slate, smelling of bleach. A clean, filthy slate. My transfer ticket was wet in my hand: Greyhound Getaways — ONE WAY/NON-REFUNDABLE.

I had stolen it from a Travelers Aid agency a year ago, a one-month pass to anywhere that Greyhound traveled in the lower forty-eight. There was nowhere I couldn't go, other than Alaska and Hawaii, and even that was temporary. Once I got to where I was going it would all come together. I would find my niche and it wouldn't involve hair, scalps, product, sales, capes, curlers, or smocks.

In this room of drawling cowboy beggars and shuffling tweakers I was feeling pretty free. It's the feeling I'd imagine having when you live on the streets, that feeling of not having to worry about bills or rent or anything but still having to keep an eye out for the man. It's not the same feeling of homelessness, but of the conscious choice to live on the streets, as dictated by the early '90s street-kid culture that pulled so many middle-class white kids from city to city, allowing them to change their names temporarily to Zeon or Anthrax or whatever their dream names had been as kids.

I always egg it on: Fate. If I had an apartment in Manhattan full of stuff to look at, I might be feeling some sense of loss. But from where I sit on this blue bench at Greyhound, there isn't a whole lot to whine about.

I heard the tinkling coming up behind me and I thought it was a dog. I could picture him padding up to me, this dog that would be my best friend and save my life, he would come bouncing around the bench, a big ball of fuzz and love. He's not much of a licker but he'll give me one quick kiss on my nose when he comes over, hops up on the bench with me and gives me a reason not to get on the bus because I Have Something To Care For.

When I turned I saw human feet, a man's two feet, each foot sporting a different color Croc shoe, but no dog. His mismatched Crocs wrapped their plastic around bright orange socks. Really bright, the socks looked terrycloth, all bumpy and pilly. Knitted.

Above the sock top came the source of the jingling of my dog-dream. Above the whole madness of two different color Crocs, Orange Socks was wearing gauze pants, sort of Hammer pants but not as low in the crotch. Baggy, though. They looked clean but old. I couldn't say as much of mine; mine were on the bad side of both age and cleanliness. Mine were dying, dead.

His were willowy, almost breathing like a hallucination, the dyes on the fabric just subtle enough to cause an optical illusion. Grey and light blue, his pants ended three inches below the knee, a half-inch above the socks. There were the bells I heard, the ones that sound like dog collar. Not jingle bells, but those Indian bells that are on bracelets at the mall's ethnic store. Like little clams only they don't open or close, just clink against each other. He had these symphonies trinkling from his hem.

The bells clinked with his every step, in a gentle way, to gentle effect. Not in a *Here I Come* way like the chirp of a ringtone splitting the silence at a movie, the user taking the call as he pushes past you to the aisle. His chimes held no such entitlement. His chimes sang, "Hi. How are ya? I'm just passin' through!" You could even tune his chimes out if you concentrated hard enough I bet.

His joypants were held up by a cord wired through the waistline. Handmade. White moppy hair curled from underneath a woven pancake hat, his sideburns became a high mass of moustache and beard, glassy white tributaries feeding this ocean of facial hair, threatening to consume his face, cover his smile. He watched me studying him. My mouth was open. He gets the looks a lot, I'm sure, but probably from asshole people that want to make fun of him. I smiled, still half-hoping that he had a dog with him, but he didn't.

More jingling came running up from behind him, a person wearing a garment that was a little louder than his pants, both literally and metaphorically. As for twinkling songs, there must have been more clamshells on her dress, or they were sewn closer together at a concentrated point of the hem.

Her dress was bright tie-dye, all primary colors swirling and choppy from the center of her sternum. It was clean and new. I couldn't see the bells but I could hear them in her long white hair, tied up somewhere in its ridiculous bun. There could have been a xylophone in there. It was beautiful, a gorgeous mass of white up above her smiling face. From her tie-dye dress, her sockless legs led to Crocs that had a tie-dye pattern on them. She was a total package. Together they were hard to look at.

They both had deep laugh lines, which is always a good sign — or at least it used to be. These days such lines are filled and eradicated before they can form: witness Taffy. The lady's laugh lines were deeper than the man's and beautiful like scars, three-inch gashes of joy that were only visible when she wasn't smiling, when her face went slack. When she smiles, the lines fill up all the way, her mouth opening wide when she begins to laugh, her eyes squinting with the deep rumble of laughter. Her smile is the opposite of Jherri's, every muscle engaged, her whole body reeling with the smile, but not creepy.

"Well-y, what're we have here, Paw?" she said to Orange Socks.

I looked up to his face, and saw that Orange Socks had a Wilford Brimley twinkle in his eye. I knew this look. It was either there to take me away or send me back. I figured he'd want nothing to do with me, this loser in a bus station. I wasn't the kid with the stick of dreams anymore, I was just the loser in the bus station. I was sure he would see that as clearly as I could.

"It's hot as Hades in here, Maw," he said, then took off his sweatshirt. Underneath the knitted poncho he wore a t-shirt, faded and peeling. It was one of his favorites; you could tell by the way he wore it and the way it fit. In heat-pressed letters spanning the length of his chest, his shirt read: Clowning Keeps Laughter Close To The Heart.

Maw whispered something into his ear, and he looked at me with a smile bigger than all the Wilford Brimleys in the world, the way I'd imagine a proud father would look at his long-lost son. As the announcements for the next departures were made, he looked at my Go Anywhere ticket and winked, the gauze of his pants and his bells dragging at me. He opened his smile again, and there were no pointy teeth.

"Ya look like you're joinin' the Circus, son."

"Yes, sir. The Circus."

His pants jingled across the room, his meaty hands dragging a few rolling cases, no doubt stuffed with wigs. Maw walked past, stopping for a second to kick me in the shoe. She looked at me, her silver hair sliding forward before being flipped behind the ear. Her eyes. For a second I feared she would ask me my name, the whole rigmarole. My adult self still worried that she was the voice of reason in this adult clown relationship, and she would hope to send me back to the prison of monotony, of scalps, of products, and the heinous Men of Cults.

"Where ya' comin' from?" She sat.

"San Francisco." When I looked at her everything spilled out. "I was a hairdresser there, I hated it, doing hair. So now I'm here."

"Well, hair, here," she said. "Tough business. My grandma was a hairdresser. Momma, too. They wanted me to do it too, but I flat refused. It used to be bad, the torture they'd put those people through. My grandma got her hair curled with a big electric spaceship!"

"A Nessler perm? The big machine?"

"I dunno what they called it, honey, but it sure sounded awful."

"It was awful," I said, "and it's only gotten worse. I'm tired. I quit."

"It's a tiresome business. And you didn't quit, honey. You moved on. Amazing the torture they put people through. They'll burn holes right through your noggin!" She knocked on her head with her left fist, three times. "Then they'll charge you for it!"

"It makes me feel itchy on the inside," I said. "I'm glad it's done."

"Well, good, uh..."

"Francis."

"Well, then... Francis. That's a beautiful name, Francis. Like Saint Francis of Assisi, you know that one? And call me Maw. None of this Ma'am stuff. I'm only seventy." Her bubble was getting as big as the room, bigger. My shell combined with hers and everything came flooding in, the bus station, the whole state of Texas even. "You know, Francis, you don't gotta stay itchy. You can always scratch."

She picked up her bags, her silver curls wrapping her strong arms like snakes, her body a mass of fannypacks and containment compartments. Zippers everywhere and twice as much Velcro. Loaded up, she walked towards the bus, kicking my bag with her Angel foot. *Push.*

Her head spun around and she caught me dead in the face. "Hey, Choo-choo, ya just gonna sit there?" And I realized she knew everything, my Most Holy Guardian Angel. She motioned to my sad bag, sitting in the grease of the loading zone. *Push.* The Greyhound door swung out with a *pssssst.* I stood, moving one foot in front of the other, pulled by the jingling hem of promises.

Acknowledgments

The author would like to thank Michelle Tea, Ali Liebegott, Beth Lisick, RADAR Productions, Beth Pickens, my fellow Lab rats, Sister Spit, Sini Anderson, Jennifer Joseph, Manic D Press, LuLu Gamma-Ray, Roxana Fausti-Arania, Josh Bonnenberg, Jane Schippers, Thor White, Shannon Williams, Zeke, and Max. With undying love to my parents and to all of my family, blood and chosen. To love.

Additional thanks to Cooper Lee Bombardier, Lindsay Brink, Mary-Rose Branchaud, James Dawson, Kristin Girard Gouhl, Dee Dee Grimes, Julie Clarke-Holman, Kathe Izzo, Jer Ber Jones, Diana and Ernie Lambert, Gabriela Laz, Paulie Maclure, George H. Reyes, Rob Schippers, Marya Schrier, Tom Studer, Tracy Minicucci, Laura Mulley, Jesse Zoldak, and Sage Botwin.

A very special Thank You to Morrisey for the title and for the songs that saved my life. They were the only ones who ever stood by me.